Praise for *From Haven to Hell*

"There are few words I can use to describe the emotional rollercoaster the second book has put me through, but dammit I would do it again!"

– Katherine Wunder (Amazon.ca)

"I loved this book even more than the first. Characters develop with more complexity as the author weaves together betrayal, insecurities, and different kinds of love. Plus, things get violent - the title is apt! I would recommend this book to young adults and older adults alike; it's an easy read that sucks you in. Can't wait for the next one!"

– Colleen (Goodreads)

"Loved diving further into the story of Clara and the Captain Duke. Finally all the chemistry between them becomes something real... And we get more glimpses into the creative historical backdrop behind the main storyline. Looking forward to the rest of this series!"

– Gurushabd (Goodreads)

"From Haven to Hell, book #2 in The Tales of the Captain Duke series, is a great read, definitely a page turner! Love how the characters evolve more in this book. Excited for Book #3 A Gentleman and a Scholar!"

– Kelly (Amazon.ca)

Also by Rebecca Diem:

Tales of the Captain Duke

The Stowaway Debutante

From Haven to Hell

A Gentleman and a Scholar *(coming soon)*

Tales of the Captain Duke

From Haven to Hell

Rebecca Diem

Eliana,
Welcome to
the Haven...
R. Diem

WOOLF LIKE ME
Publishing

Cover art by Sarah Dier-McComb
Cover design by Steve Armstrong

First Edition

Woolf Like Me Publishing
ISBN: 978-0-9938874-2-0

To the winds, to the clouds, to a life lived well,
Take me up to the sky!
To the heavens above and the land far below,
Pilot, keep to the sky!
To the sun on your face and the stars in your eyes,
Captain! Give me the sky!

Table of Contents

Chapter 1: In which our pilots attack their own

It was a fine, cloudless day. A terrible day to mount an attack from the skies. But the weather could not be helped, and the Captain Duke and his crew could not delay this dreaded moment any longer. Clara's knuckles were bone white as she clutched the railing of the airship. The land below was lush and green, with rolling hills bending into the distance, shrouded in the early morning mists. A ribbon of river could be glimpsed curving through the trees. The Lake District had always been known for its natural beauty, and now the forests and streams nestled in the valleys between the fells could be viewed in all their glory from above. Clara wished she could enjoy the scene at her leisure, but regrettably, the circumstances of their visit prohibited such sentiment. The airship was battle-ready, with armed gliders prepared to leap at a moment's notice from the bow and stern. Soon they would reach the Haven, and the battle would begin.

The Captain Duke approached the rail to stand beside her. Lost in her thoughts, she nearly jumped out of her skin as he rested a hand on her arm and pointed to steer her gaze.

"Over there, beyond those cliffs. The Haven is on an island in the Derwentwater, we'll see it soon." He looked at her with concern, "Will you be alright?"

"Yes. Just a few nerves. Tell me more. What is it like, the Haven?"

Clara was rewarded with a smile as he leaned back against the rail.

"It's an old manor house. The only one on the isle. There's thick forest on three sides with a clearing to the north for the port and cargo loaders. I found it years ago with Trick when we were looking for a place to hide out from a storm. We fixed it up, made peace with the local townsfolk. We made it into a haven. *The* Haven. Our home." He sighed, "I planned its defenses myself, and now I must exploit its weaknesses."

"Is it absolutely certain that we should expect trouble? Is there any chance that the Haven is not compromised?"

The Captain Duke stared far into the distance, gripping the railing. "A small chance, but it is not a risk we can afford. Robbie may be one of my officers, but he handpicked his crew to fly ahead. He led us into a trap."

Clara took in the view, going over the battle plan again in her mind. Hardly a week had passed since a simple raid had turned into a perilous standoff between the Captain Duke's pilots and a full complement of Tradist soldiers. She had managed to save them all by turning to the embellishments of her former life as a debutante, dressing as a highborn lady and persuading the sergeant to believe it was simply a misunderstanding. Despite the favourable ending, the incident was not without its costs. Robbie had sent them to attack that ship, and now he would answer for his betrayal.

"There. Do you see it?" he asked, leaning forward over the rail.

The Captain Duke was tense, his brow creased with worry. And yet, Clara could see his longing, his anticipation to see his home. She said nothing, but gently laid a hand over his as the island came into view. Her heart was beating quickly in her chest and she took a deep breath as the Derwentwater spread itself before them in all its splendour. The small isle in their path was charming to behold, the natural elevation according it a dramatic flair as it rose above the deep blue waves.

"You should go below," he said after a moment. "Nessa will be attempting her escape."

Clara couldn't help the smirk that crossed her face, but was reassured by his matching smile. She squeezed his hand, "There's still hope."

The Captain Duke's smile faded and he grew serious once more.

"Tend to Nessa. She needs your care."

Clara wished that she could ease his fears. He stood before her with his hair unbound, fiery waves that were swept across his shoulders by the wind. She fought an urge to tuck one of the bright strands behind his ear and tell him everything would turn out fine. Instead, she gave a curt nod, and after one final look at the scene before her, Clara descended to the cabins below.

Opening the door, Clara discovered her patient had indeed escaped the bed. Nessa was leaning against the wall, clutching the edge of the windowpane that faced the isle.

"Oh, Nessa. Not on my watch. Back to bed."

"Cruel mistress, let me get a glimpse of my Haven, my home."

Clara smiled at the melodramatics. Nessa's jovial mood was a great improvement over the pale and silent woman that had terrified them only days before. Nessa had a large, ugly welt on the side of her head from the bungled raid. Even a fighter such as Nessa could not hold against those odds. The captain of the other airship had knocked her unconscious with a blow to the temple and Clara had feared the worst. Mercifully, Nessa was recovering from the ordeal, but it would be awhile before the piratess was battle-ready once more.

When Nessa first woke, groggy and confused, she had nearly knocked herself out again trying to fight her way out of the medic's quarters. Clara was moved to tears by her friend's frantic struggles as she screamed and swore vengeance on any and all that brought harm to her crew. Only Trick had been able to calm her, whispering in her ear and stroking her hair as the others held her still. Now that the danger had passed, Clara was tasked with keeping her abed. The assignment was proving to be a difficult one.

"Why are we spinning?" Nessa groaned after Clara helped her back to the cot and tucked her in. She sank back into the pillows, clutching at the bandages wrapped around her head. Clara prepared a fresh cloth and brought it over to her bedside.

"We're not spinning, you are. Now lie still, Nurse Susan said you were concussed. You need to rest." Nessa lay still and allowed Clara to spread the cool cloth across her forehead. It would be at least another week before the dizzy spells would fade completely.

"Are you sure this is doing any good? Doesn't she have

some concoction to make this spell go away?"

"The cloth is for your comfort. Rest is what your head needs to heal. The bruises are fading at least; they look much better today."

"Liar," Nessa muttered.

Clara smiled, but did not deny it. In truth, the deep purple bruising that blossomed the day after the raid had turned to an ugly, mottled yellow. Still, she was looking much improved since gaining consciousness only six days earlier. Nessa fussed with her covers and reached down to check her pistols. She caught Clara's glance.

"I just like to be prepared, that's all."

"Nessa, in your current state *I* am likely a better shot than you."

"We'll start your training at the Haven. I'll make a decent pilot out of you yet."

At that moment, hollers from above announced their impending arrival. Clara ran to a porthole to peer out at the island below. She watched the gliders launch themselves from the airship and disappear into the distance.

"Tell me what's happening. Tell me everything," called Nessa from the bed.

"The gliders are circling. They're dropping the powders. I can see blue smoke through the trees."

"Ah, Madge's smoke bombs. A good choice, that will leave them scrambling."

Clara shifted, craning for a better view, "I can—I think I can see it. We're getting close, I can see the tops of the gables but the smoke is too thick. How will we land in this?"

"The smoke is heavy; it will settle and spread out soon. It's enough to confuse a man, but the airship will be able to navigate above."

"Yes, you're right. It's getting clearer now." Clara pressed her nose against the pane of glass, "They're descending the ropes!"

She could just barely make out the figures as the pilots rappelled down the side of the airship—past the scrolling that named it the *Robin's Egg* now—before using a system of ropes and knots to quickly lower themselves to the ground. They disappeared into the smoke below. All she could see was swirling blue clouds and tree tops at first, then the upper floor of the manor came into view.

The exterior was old and crumbling, but the Haven retained its former grandeur. Two large wings flanked the main house, complete with gabled windows. Clara could see at least six chimneys, and large pane-glass windows hinted at a ballroom or observatory in the southern wing. More of its features were revealed, window by window, floor by floor. It was a surreal sight, a crumbling palace rising up from cobalt blue fog.

As the smoke dissipated, she caught sight of Anderssen, the tallest of the Captain Duke's pilots. His bald head shone with perspiration as he struggled with another man. Soon she spotted the Captain Duke at the Haven's entrance. He threw a half-dressed man down the front stairway, shouting something indiscernible. The pilot Madge appeared out of the mists and threw down another pouch from the collection tied about her waist, clearing the air in a large radius around her. More pilots emerged from the smoke, some hauling their compatriots and forcing them to sit in a row.

"I think they've rounded them up. Is it safe now? Is it over?"

Nessa let out a deep breath but her anxiety was apparent, "We should be down there for this."

Just then, Cat bounded into the room. She too had been forced to watch from above. The teenaged girl and her younger brother, Mouse, were not yet allowed to join in the battles, though they had spent their lives on airships and their knowledge likely surpassed that of every member of the crew save for the Captain Duke and his officers, Trick and Nessa.

"Trick got the signal, we're going to dock the airship."

Clara and Nessa exchanged a look.

"Well, ready to see your new home away from home?" said Nessa, attempting to stand before sitting back heavily on the bed.

"Nessa, perhaps you should stay here and rest."

It only took one glare for Clara to gather a compress and fix Nessa's bandages before buckling her father's ancient dueling pistols around her waist and heading to the top deck to assist. The ropes and gears were familiar to her now, but she had never actually docked an airship before. The other pilots moved around the ship with ease, going from one duty to the next in a familiar dance as the airship slowly sank towards the earth. She followed Trick's instructions as he manoeuvered into position, climbing over the starboard side to a rope ladder. When she reached the end, she swung back and forth until she could jump on to the dock. She pulled on the ropes and lashed the end of the ladder to the heavy beams, creating a bridge as the galley floated down to her level. More ropes were thrown down to pilots waiting below and they secured the airship on all sides. The vessel was sheltered from changeable winds by the nearby cliffs and tall trees and was bobbing gently in the breeze as Trick helped Nessa cross to the port, followed by Cat and Mouse.

The tallport was nested in a large clearing north of the Haven with layers of spokes arranged around a curved stair. Three other ships were already docked, tethered to the ground with large iron rings embedded deep within the earth. Two were smaller models, one made of lightweight wood and another with bright brass finishings that gleamed in the light; but Clara recognized the third. It was the merchant vessel she'd run away on. She laughed at the sight of it, recalling the surprise of Nessa and Trick when they had found her hiding in the cargo hold. Barely a moon's turn later and it felt like a lifetime ago. She remembered sitting crouched behind the crates, armed with only a crowbar as the pirates took the ship. She remembered how her heart had nearly leapt from her chest as she revealed herself to Trick and Nessa. She remembered her first sight of the Captain Duke and how she had talked her way into joining his crew. Thanks to the merchant captain's scheming, Trick and Nessa had nearly killed them all. If Clara hadn't been snooping, they may never have discovered that the hold was packed to the brim with gunpowder instead of the far less incendiary grain they were expecting.

"You've come a long way, Clara, my dear," said Trick, grinning from ear to ear as they joined her.

"Quite. Whatever became of all that gunpowder?" she asked.

"I imagine it's still aboard. Safer up here, away from the

Haven."

"Ah, yes." Clara viewed the airship with apprehension, wiping her palms against her borrowed trousers.

"Never fear, my dear. First we'll deal with Robbie, then the Captain will decide how best to rid ourselves of our combustible cargo."

Satisfied, Clara took Nessa's other arm. She had no idea what they would encounter below, but she was beginning to take an odd comfort in the unknown. Her unexpected adventure had proven to be quite beyond her imagination.

Chapter 2: In which our hero confronts a traitor

The Captain Duke was very nearly trembling from the adrenaline in his veins. It had been a brief skirmish, but he was certain there must be more to the situation than what he could observe. Most of Robbie's crew surrendered as soon as they realised they were defending the Haven from their own. Many were nursing sore heads from being knocked about, but he guessed that much of their discomfort was due to the effects of late night revelry. He made a note to thank Trick for timing their arrival with the dawn.

He glared at the man who sat, bound and gagged, in front of the Haven's steps. Robbie was half-dressed and red-eyed, his pale hair hanging limp and tangled around his face. It was clear that he had woken mid-attack. The Captain Duke had found him stumbling down the hall. If he was not already furious over the circumstances of the failed raid, he would be feeling positively lethal over the lack of defenses.

It was almost like a scene from a faerie tale of old with the wisps of blue smoke dissipating at the treeline, stirred into clouds as the remainder of his crew joined them, Cat and Mouse leading the way. Cat's expression was serious, still a child but beyond her years in wisdom. Her younger brother had all the innocence of youth, bounding ahead with an ever-present smile, until a stern comment from Cat made him pause to wait for the others to catch up. Trick, a head shorter than his companions, was doing his best to support Nessa with assistance from Clara. At the sight of them, Robbie struggled to speak through his gag, observing Nessa with some distress.

"Quiet. You will have ample opportunity to speak soon enough."

When all the pilots had gathered, he gestured to Anderssen to unbind the gag. Robbie wiped the spittle from his mouth on one shoulder.

"What happened?" he croaked. He looked up at the assembly, as though searching for some clue, "Captain, please. Tell me what has transpired."

"I think you know."

Robbie prostrated himself before them, "Truly, I do not. Please, Captain, I swear it. I don't know what you have heard but it has clearly put my loyalty in question. What is the cause of this? Who injured Nessa?"

The Captain Duke remained silent as he watched the blonde man's discomfort. His crew shifted from foot to foot, faces lined with tension and fingers twitching towards their own weapons.

"Captain," Robbie said as he struggled to one knee. He bowed his head, "I know not what I have done to merit such distrust. My life, as always, is in your hands. If I have wronged you, please tell me what I must do as restitution."

"Quit the dramatics, Robbie," said Nessa, as she moved to stand nearer. Clara stayed by her side, supporting her. Nessa's voice was tight and edged in shades of explosive rage, "That shipment you led us to, it was guarded by a full complement of bloody soldiers. We barely escaped with our lives."

The Captain felt an electric current run down his spine at the memory of the moment he saw his friend fall on the decks, his fear that she was lost.

Robbie had sat down again in apparent shock, "Impossible! My sources said–"

"You doubt me?"

"No, Nessa! I– please, sir, let me get to the bottom of this. I swear I will. I had no idea."

"Enough," said the Captain Duke.

Despite her concussion, Nessa was near to tearing the man's head off. Robbie switched tactics, turning to face the Captain Duke with a look of penitence.

"I have been at your side for six years, Captain. I would never—never—deliberately endanger our crew. Please, believe me."

The man looked stricken. Robbie's concern seemed genuine, but the Captain Duke could no longer trust him. He knew his guile. It was useful when employed against their enemies, but he was dismayed to be receiving the same treatment. He grabbed Robbie's shirt and hauled him to his feet.

"You swear you had no knowledge of the soldiers?"

"No, sir."

The Captain shoved him towards the manor. "You will provide us with a full account of what transpired. Every damned detail. And you are hereby stripped of your duties as an officer." He turned to the others, "We will continue this discussion inside. The rest of you, tend to the ship."

Trick began shouting orders for the crew to unload the airship and tend to their duties. A low buzz permeated the clearing. Whispered breaths exchanging rumour and speculation. The Captain Duke ignored them. He was more concerned with the pallor of Nessa's face. Clara seemed to be supporting her full weight as they moved towards the steps.

"I think I need to lie down," Nessa said as her knees buckled.

"Help me!" Clara called out, struggling to hold the tall woman upright.

The Captain reached them in three steps, sweeping Nessa into his arms to carry her into the manor. Ashen-faced, Nessa cradled her brow in pain as she leaned against his chest. Her lack of protest at being carried like a babe frightened him. Clara hurried to open the door ahead of them.

Racing through the gallery to his study off the main hall, the Captain directed Clara to clear a stack of maps and books off a long sofa opposite the fireplace. He lowered Nessa onto the seat as Cat and Mouse entered on their heels.

"Water and cloths, now," he ordered.

Clara fussed with Nessa's bandages while the Captain Duke looked around the room with displeasure. The many shelves of books and maps were relatively undisturbed, but there were dirty boot prints on his desk, one of his two grand armchairs had been removed from its usual place by the hearth, and the side table he usually kept stocked with a fine scotch now held an empty decanter. He added that to his list of Robbie's sins. Within minutes, Mouse returned to set a bowl on a nearby table and Cat ran in with a clean sheet and set at it with the small dagger she wore at her side. Clara wet the cloths with the cool water and began to dab at Nessa's brow. As Nessa's colour returned, the Captain thanked them and sent them out to their duties before Trick entered with Robbie in tow.

"What happened, Ness?" Robbie asked, crossing the room toward them. One look from the Captain stopped him in his tracks. Nessa opened her eyes to match his glare.

"What do you think happened, Robbie? There were consequences. We were damned lucky to escape," she said, she shut her eyes again, leaning into Clara's ministrations.

"Ness, I am so sorry. The Tradists have been guarding their shipments closely this year. Are you badly hurt?"

"Hurt?" her eyes flew open, "You have the audacity–"

The Captain set a hand on her shoulder to prevent Nessa from rising to tear into the pale man, but she continued to speak in deadly tones, "You knew the shipments were being guarded, Robert Codswaddle. They damn near killed us. Your job was to avoid incidents exactly such as this."

"I swear, I didn't know!"

The Captain's temper broke, "It was your job to know. We trusted your information. We trusted you." His voice rang with fury.

"Captain, please!" called Clara.

He turned at Clara's interruption with a look that would make brave men cower. Clara glared and dampened the cloth.

"Captain, the shouting is hurting her."

Nessa massaged her temple, "Oh please, don't stop on my account. But as much as I am enjoying this little chat, I think it's time for me to rest."

The Captain softened, "Will you be alright?"

"It is only a headache. The dizzy spell has passed. Clara can help me up to my rooms."

He helped her rise and the two women made to leave the room. Robbie inserted himself between them and the door, stumbling slightly as his hands were still bound behind his back.

"Get out of my way," Nessa said through gritted teeth.

"Ness, please, I cannot undo the results of my negligence, but I swear on my life I will make amends. Please tell me if there is anything I might do to speed your recovery. I will be wretched forever if you do not forgive me."

"Then you are a wretch," she said, continuing towards the door.

"Come now, none were lost. I had faith in the competence of our crew to handle a few guards. I did not anticipate the soldiers, but still you managed to defeat them. Do not tell me my confidence was misplaced."

The Captain felt disgust coil in his stomach at the sight of Robbie's attempt to charm his way out of trouble. The pirate was charismatic and well-liked by the crew, an asset that was now a liability. Before, Nessa and Robbie would have argued long into the night about this or that, often at odds but always collegial. Now, she regarded him with a loathing compounded by his role in her current state of weakness.

"If Clara hadn't intervened, we would be dead or worse right now," she responded.

"Then you have my gratitude, Clara. I am your eternal servant," he said, bowing to her. "I don't believe we have met."

Clara lifted her chin and glared, infusing her narrowed eyes and upright bearing with all the censure and judgement of her true class. The Captain could not help his smirk. He watched with great pleasure as Robbie faltered under her icy scowl. *A fearsome lass, that one*, he thought.

"This is our stowaway, Robbie. She managed to save our skins twice while your ineptitude nearly cost us everything. We are all in her debt," said the Captain. He turned to the women, "Go. Rest. I will look in once we are finished here."

The Captain Duke closed the door after them and took a moment to compose himself before turning. If it were any other pilot he would have them taken care of immediately. Robbie was too great a liability. He had been a leader and the trusted confidante of many. The Captain needed time to gather more evidence, but time could work in the other man's favour as well. He knew Robbie's dramatics were intended to shore up his support among the crew. The man was a good actor. It was difficult even for the Captain to know when he was being genuine, and he had known him for years. If Robbie was a traitor, the Captain had a much larger problem on his hand than just one disgruntled pilot. Robbie would not act alone. He needed to determine the extent to which their operation was compromised, and find out how much Robbie's "sources" knew. For now, the Captain Duke decided that Robbie needed to be reminded why he was not a man to be trifled with.

"I watched them strike her," he said, still facing the heavy door. "I watched her fall. I thought she was dead."

He turned, allowing his rage free reign. "I watched the battle turn against our crew in an instant, and I knew, I *knew*, that we were all lost."

"And yet, we prevailed," Robbie swallowed. "We always prevail."

"No. *We* only prevail when we can count on each other. I can no longer count on you. We escaped by whatever divine intervention delivered Clara to our airship. Without her we would all be dead or imprisoned at this moment." He walked to his desk and leaned against it, crossing his arms. "Ease my suspicions, Robbie. Seasons of successful raids and the one that fails disastrously just happens to occur when you and the crewmembers you selected were safely away."

"Captain, I have served you loyally for years. Can one error undo all our history together? A grave error, I admit, and I feel it acutely. Let me help you. I will find the source of the misinformation. Tell me what I can do to regain your confidence."

The Captain looked to Trick, silent and watchful, sitting in the corner of the room.

"Well, what do you think?"

"I think we should hang him."

The Captain watched with amusement as the blood drained entirely from Robbie's already pale complexion.

After a long pause, Trick continued, "But, if he is not a traitor, we would do well to accept his aid. Give him the opportunity to prove himself an honest man. If he fails, he'll answer to my sword."

The Captain Duke approached the quaking man, unsheathing his knife. "Very well. Robbie, you have one week and you will be watched. I'm certain you understand the consequences should you attempt any escape." He turned the man around to cut his bindings. Leaning in to Robbie's ear, he spoke in a low voice edged with thunder, "Leave us."

"Thank you, sir. Thank you, Captain."

Visibly shaking with relief, Robbie turned to exit the room. When he opened the door, the frame was filled by Anderssen's towering form. The Captain Duke nodded, and he escorted Robbie away, closing the door behind them.

The Captain Duke sighed and sank down onto the sofa, leaning back and running his hands through his hair. Trick came over to lean against the mantle opposite him.

"I am getting too old for this, Trick."

The older man laughed, "Nonsense."

"I am not as young as I was when we started this. It's been how long—a decade now? The risks weigh heavier on my mind with each season. There are times I find myself longing for the storm season to begin so we may rest."

"And you're a better Captain for it. You care for your pilots and the crew sees it. They will follow you. This conflict with Robbie will blow over one way or another. We've been through far worse."

"Are you never tired of it all?"

"Ah, Captain. I was tired before I ever met you. And then one day this flame-haired snip of a boy stole half a dozen crates of taters from right under my nose. I was ready to strip his hide when I tracked him down. But then I found him handing out the goods to a gaggle of orphans in an alleyway. Do you remember what happened next?"

He laughed, "I nearly pissed myself when you cornered us."

"And you pulled out your pocketknife, stood your ground, said food belonged to those who needed it most. I believe you made some rather strong statements about my weight at the time as well."

"The Tradists let you go soft." The Captain Duke smiled, "I thought you would beat me, and instead you joined me."

"You inspired me, Captain. You inspire the crew. Good men grow tired but they must go on." Trick rubbed the greying whiskers of his dark beard, "You ought to find someone to bring back that fire."

The Captain Duke snorted. But then he sat back and considered Trick's words. He had been a wild little thing, angered by the injustice he had seen around him. Trick had found him, guided him, supported him in becoming the man he was today. They always navigated the difficult choices together. He did not need to bear the burden alone.

“The raids are becoming a problem. We need a better plan if we are to continue. They’re catching on to us,” he said.

“I know it. Any ideas?”

“Clara had one. She suggested we pretend to be inspectors, target the ports. Take a little from each shipment, but not enough for anyone to take notice. Issue receipts of inspection and the like.”

“Bold as brass, that one. It could work.”

“We’d need disguises. But if she is able to pull it off it would reduce the risk to our crew.”

“Consider it. I think it’s a good plan. We should take a week here at least to allow Nessa to recover. We can gather information and supplies while we wait. Take Clara to see Mrs. Cottingham in town; she’s rather clever with a needle and thread. You can stop in and have a word with Tims at the store. See if he or the others have heard anything about the Tradists’ plans. And take some of the grain with you. They will not be expecting us this time of year.”

“Very well. I’ll go to town tomorrow. But if we are to embark on this new strategy, I’d like to keep the information close. I don’t trust Robbie and we cannot risk a leak. We need to watch the crew and see how they respond to him.”

“Agreed. I’ll sound out some of his people, see where their loyalties lie.”

The Captain and Trick worked out a rough plan for the week and what needed to be done in preparation. Repairs and maintenance on the ships, an inventory of the goods, research into the ports they would target, and all the logistics involved in hosting a full crew of pilots and keeping them occupied for the week. When the Captain Duke rose to leave, Trick stopped him once more.

"Remember your purpose here, Captain. Do not be discouraged by one man's weakness."

The Captain Duke nodded, no further words were needed between the two men. They had seen far too much together for any mere declaration of thanks to be sufficient. The Captain left the room reassured of his purpose, ready to face this and any other challenge to come his way.

Chapter 3: In which our heroine explores her new home

Clara supported Nessa as they slowly made their way back through the gallery to the stairs. She had barely noticed the oak panelled walls in their earlier rush. Now she took the time to appreciate her surroundings. Lush occasional chairs and small tables dotted the hall and the landing as they made their way up a grand curved staircase to the second floor. The brass was tarnished and the paintings worn, but light streamed in through tall windows. Faded damask fabric hinted at a former glory, now settled into comfortable squalor in its senescence. The manor carried itself with the impression of stateliness, humble in its decline. They continued down a hall and turned a corner into what she guessed was the east wing by the angle of the light.

"Three doors down on the right," said Nessa, massaging her head with her free hand.

The door opened to a well-appointed room with large windows that looked out on to the forest. The glass had been scrubbed recently enough, and the room showed signs that great care had been taken to make it comfortable. It might have been a ladies' dayroom in a previous life. Now it contained a pleasant jumble of mismatched furniture. Cozy armchairs and a chaise longue were scattered around the largest windows as a sort of parlour area. In the adjoining room, a large poster bed and wardrobe dominated the space.

"There's an empty room next to mine if you like. It's just through that door," Nessa pointed.

"Do all pilots have their own quarters here?"

"Not all, some prefer to share. But the officers have first pick and there are plenty of empty rooms for the taking."

Clara found extra pillows in the wardrobe and made sure Nessa was comfortable in her bed with a good view of the outside. She made herself busy airing out the chests and opening windows while her friend rested. She had done without a lady's maid for most of her life, preferring to manage her own affairs. Only recently had she made use of one, with all the balls and events she'd had to attend since her entrance into society. A different life, she reminded herself. No need to think on it any longer. She opened the door to the next room and found a charming bedroom with pale green papered walls. She unfastened the shutters and raised the pane to let the breeze blow into the room, allowing herself to enjoy the brush of morning air as she removed the dust cloths from the furniture. Her reverie was interrupted by a creak from the floorboards in the hall.

After a moment of alarm as her door slowly squeaked open, Clara let out a sigh of relief at the sight of Cat's golden-brown curls peeking around the frame.

"You startled me," she whispered at the girl.

"Sorry!" she whispered back.

With a significant glance in the direction of the room where Nessa slept, she closed the door while Cat bounced over to the bed.

"So this is your room now? It's nice. Some are a bit

musty, but this one will do. You can choose any you like you know. There's lots of 'em."

"Where is yours?"

"Mine is up in the Bird's Nest," she said, beaming with pride. "It's upstairs in the gable by the big oak tree. You can come and see it sometime if you like."

"I would like that very much," Clara said.

"How's Nessa?"

"Better. Too much activity, I suppose. Her vision does seem much clearer, and she has regained most of her balance as well. She does not enjoy being an invalid."

Cat laughed, "I hope she's better soon. It's almost harvest season, and we ought to be out and robbing the Tradists."

"The last raid was so violent. I'm surprised you have an appetite for it."

The young girl's expression changed, her usual bright and open demeanor becoming more guarded. She frowned and stared out the window, silent. Clara felt terrible immediately after speaking.

"Cat, I am so sorry. I did not mean to judge. It's just not something I am accustomed to. I would just be heartbroken if any harm came to you."

"I can take care of myself, and Mouse too. I've been doing it since I was a babe."

"I have no doubt of your capabilities. But the Haven would be a lovely place to grow up. Why does the Captain bring you along on these dangerous pursuits if there is an alternative?"

"Well, for one, Mouse and I hate being landlocked. It would be so terribly boring. And Captain would never leave us behind. He swore that he would never." A bright, hard anger lit Cat's eyes, "The Tradists took our family. And I will make them pay for it."

In that moment, Clara could see the indomitable force Cat would become when she was grown. She was fearless, courageous, and her loyalty was absolute. For now, though, she was still a girl. Clara drew her into a hug, "They ought to quake in their beds at night."

Cat rewarded her with a small smile, but Clara knew she needed to do more to make up for her errant comment.

"I think Nessa will sleep for some time. Will you show me your Bird's Nest? And perhaps the rest of the manor? I trust that you know every nook and cranny."

The young pilot beamed at that. After checking on Nessa and receiving an affirmative murmur that she was content, the two of them went to explore.

Clara was charmed by her new home, from the small green apples growing in the orchard and the blue waves lapping at the shores of their oasis, to the myriad of rooms filled with curiosities from around the world. They first ascended a hidden stairwell to the top of the gable that was Cat's home. It was a cozy little space, filled with personal treasures that she was eager to show. A blue flower of blown glass sat amidst jewelry and other baubles. A small book of poetry with exquisite binding was laid atop a messy pile of books. A woven plaid blanket covered the narrow bed, topped with a well-loved doll. And naturally, amidst these facets of girlhood, there was also an impressive display of weaponry. Swords hung neatly on the wall, a few pistols and gleaming blades. It amused Clara to note the care that was taken to clean and store these items in comparison to the mess of clothes spilling out of a trunk in the corner. Cat was certain to grow into an interesting sort of woman, the likes of which had yet to be seen by this world.

Then Cat dashed over to her window and climbed out, beckoning Clara to follow. Swallowing uncertainty, she followed the girl out onto shaky tiles to stand at the apex of the roof, clinging to the iron work. The view was spectacular. The hills of the Derwentwater curved around them, just visible above the trees. In the far distance they could just catch a glimpse of the tiny specks of airships travelling the trade routes on the way north to Scotland. Cat told her tale after tale of their exploits and close escapes.

"But what of the local residents? Surely they must know of this place by now?"

"Oh, of course. But we never attack the routes near our home, and Captain has made arrangements with the merchants of Keswick in exchange for their loyalty and protection. It's important to make good allies. That's what Captain and Trick say."

As Clara listened, the young pilot grew in her estimation. Her age had little effect on her wealth of experience. She was a clever girl, quick to learn and always drawing lessons from her environment, watching those she admired with an intense focus. In many ways she was already an adult, and yet she managed to retain a youthful delight about her world. She was a survivor. Clara wondered if someday she might learn more about the tragedy that set her and her brother on this course, but thought it best to let Cat decide when to confide in her.

Returning inside, they made their way through the manor. The kitchens were spacious and friendly. Cook and Peg were bustling about, happy to prepare food with a real stove. The dining hall was large, rows of tables lined the walls, with a larger table on the dais at the head of the room. There was a parlour that had been repurposed as a lounge for darts and other amusements, a pantry turned into weapons storage, a gallery filled with portraits of nameless strangers from long forgotten eras, and an endless number of rooms adapted to the purposes of a transient pirate crew. It amused Clara to be surrounded by such familiar trappings made unfamiliar in their new incarnation. She felt embraced by the manor's strange duality.

Cat saved her favourite room for last, pushing through a grand set of double doors to reveal a large ballroom. The midday light slanted through windows that stretched up into the second storey, illuminating the inlaid design of the parquet floors and the faded artwork that graced the walls. Dust motes danced to an invisible orchestra. The fearsome Cat transformed into a young girl once more, twirling to the center of the room and tumbling to stretch out on the sunlit floor.

"One day we're going to have a ball in here, and everyone will dance. We'll have fiddles and flutes and everything Trick can find to play and it will be a party like none have seen before, and everyone will come from far and wide to visit."

Clara came to sit in the patch of light beside her friend. "It sounds lovely. But these things are best when shared with friends, not strangers."

"Have you been to a ball?"

She sighed, "Yes. A number of them."

"What was it like? Did you wear a beautiful dress and dance all night? Did they have those tiny sparkling glasses? Who played the music?"

She smiled at the young girl's curiosity.

"Well…" she started before frowning.

How could she explain to Cat the joy and wonder of that first ball without mention of the ugliness that followed as consequence. She too had waited, breathless with anticipation, for her first ball. She too had spent weeks preparing and practicing, a model student for her etiquette instructor Miss Ellington for perhaps the first time in her life. A new gown for the occasion, hair curled into delicate ringlets, her father beaming as he escorted her down the staircase. Even then his arm had been frail beneath her hand, and she cherished the memory of dancing with him. Her dance card was filled with young gentlemen from the best families on the Isle of Wight, many of whom she remembered playing with as a child. And one charming, raven-haired man had stood out from the rest. Clara shuddered at the thought of the course her life might have taken, and rolled onto her side to look at Cat.

"I think a ball here at the Haven would be far superior to any that I have attended," she said, turning her mind from the matter.

The two stayed in the grand hall until the bell rang for the midday meal, dreaming up plans and giggling at the images they conjured of their formidable crew in pearls and tails. Clara lingered on the thought of the Captain Duke dressed in finery and wondered which of the rumours held any truth about his upbringing. Perhaps he had attended his share of balls as well. She dusted off her clothes and went to fetch a tray for Nessa while Cat bounded ahead, a stomach on two legs whenever there was food. She thought that balls belonged to the past she had left behind, but who knew what her future might hold?

Chapter 4: In which our hero speaks of gunpowder, treason and plot

The Captain woke from an uneasy slumber. The first day had been a tense affair. He watched the assembled pilots, sharing stories as they caught up on the events of the past few weeks. To all but the closest observer, there was no discernible resentment for the attack earlier in the day. The mercenary nature of the pirates' work meant they tended to be quick to forgive, but rarely forgot a slight. But the Captain could see the tight smiles that did not reach the eyes, laughter that was too loud and long, and a stiffness to their engagements that was not there before. He would need to be cautious. He needed to ensure there were no traitors among his crew to jeopardize future raids; the safety of his pilots was paramount. The Captain had reached out to a trusted few earlier in the day, requesting that they keep their ears open for any signs of dissent. He sent word around that they would rest at the Haven while Nessa recovered, but truly he wanted time to sort out the mess created by Robbie and discover the loyalties of his men. One bad apple could turn the barrel.

He ate a small breakfast in the kitchen as the cooks prepared for the day's meals. He would visit the town today for fresh supplies. It seemed that most of Robbie's time had been spent drinking and carousing. After touring the storerooms and checking in with Trick, he had a long list of needed items.

The Captain took a tray of food for Nessa on his way up to ask what she required from the town. Clara answered his knock.

"Oh! Good morning, Captain."

"Ah, Clara, good morning. Is Nessa awake?"

"I am. Come in, that smells delicious," Nessa called from her bed.

"Feeling better today?"

"The solid ground is doing my head well. You were right, Captain. It will be good to rest a little. But you should fly out sooner than later, do not delay on my account."

"Nonsense. It suits my purpose for us to remain here for the week. We need to assess the situation before we proceed."

She sighed, folding her arms, "I wish I could be of more help."

"You can begin by adding to our list. I'll be making a trip to the town today."

Nessa perused the list, commenting on this and that and adding her own notes as Clara busied herself about the room.

"I'll need a new set of trousers if you don't mind stopping in to see Mrs. Cottingham. She has my measurements."

"Indeed. I'm of a mind to take Cat and Mouse to see her. The pair of them are growing like weeds," said the Captain. He turned to Clara, "Will you join us? I thought we could discuss that idea of yours."

"Oh, yes!" Nessa's eyes twinkled, "Clara, go with them. You could use some new clothes. You can't very well wear my hand-me-downs forever."

"Oh, I don't mind at all," Clara protested.

"Please, how many times have you rolled up the hem on those? You need something to fit you properly for gliding. And if we're to pull off that scheme of yours, pretending to be inspectors, you'll need an outfit to go along with the ruse."

"Well, if it isn't any trouble…"

"I insist," said the Captain.

The Captain Duke didn't mind the excuse to spend more time in her company, though Anderssen and a few of the cook's assistants would be joining them as well. With a mock bow he left Clara to gather her things and meet them in the clearing while he sought out the children.

The group took one of the smaller airships to town, the *Zephyr*. It was a sleek brass vessel with an air of respectability, a balloon of deep midnight, and a brand new gyrometric steering system. The Captain Duke's second favourite, after his own of course. He enjoyed airships like this one, with all their cogs and gears exposed. It was a wondrous thing to see the mechanics of the flight out where one and all could see their function; he much preferred these more recent designs. Easier to maintain, and better for a pirate's purpose to customize to one's liking. It was a good size, but could not hold a full complement of his crew and cargo, so the *Zephyr* was mostly used for shorter trips and covert missions.

Anderssen stood tall at the stern, watching for signs of trouble. The Captain Duke could see how well the crew regarded the tall, quiet pilot, and was considering him to replace the disgraced Robbie as an officer. Cat and Mouse had the run of the *Zephyr* and were currently perched high above in some rigging. Not for the first time did he wonder whether the two siblings had ever indeed spent significant time on the ground during their young lives. Clara joined him at the bow to discuss her idea to trick the Tradist merchants out of their goods.

"We'll need a better idea of the spoilage ratios for different goods to avoid raising suspicion. And examples of receipts. We can make our own. Of course they'll be incredibly beneficial to our own recordkeeping as well."

"I believe I have some books on the subject if you wish to study the matter further. They're in my study at the Haven," he said, laughing at how the suggestion made her brown eyes crinkle with delight. "One would think you were a bluestocking, not a reformed debutante."

"I'm learning I can be all of many things. A lady and a hellcat, Nessa says. Might as well add bluestocking to the mix. Soon I'll have as many identities as you."

"You're in good company."

Clara smiled at that before continuing to outline her plan, "So, I think we should have a central command structure and break into smaller teams to cover the ports in one area at a time. An inspector, a guard and two porters, perhaps. Enough to be legitimate but small enough to disappear if things go sideways…"

The Captain Duke listened, interjecting only when necessary. Something new and unexpected was exactly what the situation called for. It gave him hope that his crew could find a way out of their troubles and thrive.

They docked the *Zephyr* at the small port on the north shore of the Derwentshire, coming in low to tether it to one of the spokes. Keswick's tower had only one layer of docks; the bulk of the trading vessels still favoured the main routes along the coasts. Old habits, the Captain Duke supposed, but the inland towns were beginning to grow and flourish with the increased access provided by the advances in travel and shipment by air. Its mark could be seen on Keswick itself, with new mechanical cabs to transport goods about town, great-geared bicycles rode by men and women alike, and small turbines on most of the houses to generate light. The merchants were selling wares from disparate places, things the elders of the town had only dreamed of seeing in their lifetimes. Children played with clockwork toys, flocking like sparrows as they chased wind-up gliders through the streets. A tidy, pleasant town.

As they set off walking the familiar streets, each to their own task, his spirits lifted. Much of the progress was due to the patronage of the Captain Duke and his crew. It was good to see the effects of their work so apparent, to see a town flourish as it returned to prosperity. Cat and Mouse were busy pointing out all their favourite shops to Clara. All who saw them tipped their hats in greeting. Many times their progress was halted by the need to exchange news and good mornings with the townsfolk. The Captain Duke made sure to ask after family members by name and ensure that he was up to date on the affairs of the town. It was good policy to remain on friendly terms with those he relied on for their loyalty and protection, but it was an easy affair among such genuinely pleasant people.

They made their way to the clothier's shop just off the main street. The dressmaker, Mrs. Cottingham, looked up as they entered, and clapped her hands in surprise.

"Bless me! If it isn't the dear Captain Duke! And Cat! And Mouse! Goodness, Molly, just look at how our wee pilots have grown." She gestured to her assistant, "Come now, dears, Molly will take your measure."

The Captain Duke introduced Clara and explained their needs. Mouse begged to go first so he could accompany the Captain on his errands.

"We'll need at least one set for the inspector's uniform. That design I shall leave to your judgement. And two more sets for daily use."

Clara pulled him aside, "Captain, I—I have a matter of delicacy to discuss."

He raised an eyebrow, but listened.

"I have some coin on me, but—but I must confess, I have never handled it in a store," she blushed.

He struggled to maintain his composure. Laughter would not help matters one bit in this instance. It was not customary for any person of stature to handle their own finances, let alone a young lady of good breeding. It was all done by accounts sent around monthly to the houses, or by one's staff.

"Really, Clara. It is no matter. Of course we have an account for the Haven here."

"Please, I have my own funds. I would prefer it."

He considered the merit in arguing with her and grinned.

"Your services have proven very valuable to our crew.

Please consider this a gesture of thanks," he said, placing a hand at the small of her back. He enjoyed the way her breath caught at his touch. "You have earned my gratitude, Clara. Take advantage of it."

Mouse only had to be reprimanded for fidgeting twice as he stood and endured the measurements. The seamstress was rewarded with a wide smile when she finished her work.

"Off with you now. Good lad," Molly said as she patted him on his head. Cat jumped onto the stool and spread her arms.

"I'll leave her to you, Clara," said the Captain. "We'll return in an hour."

He quickly left the store with Mouse and Anderssen. He watched through the window as, with sudden realization, Clara searched her pockets for the change purse that had been hidden within.

It was gone. She looked up and caught his laugh as he shook the small purse at her through the window before walking down the street. His mood was already much improved by the trip to town.

The three of them made their way to a general store run by the head of the local merchants' association, entering the bright and friendly storefront to the scent of spices and fresh goods. The crates and shelves were organized and neat, and the long counter gleamed.

"Hello, Master Tims."

"Captain! How wonderful to see you. I heard word that you were sighted in town. We did not expect your return for another month at the least."

"We hit a spot of trouble and had to return earlier than anticipated. It's no matter. We'll be up and flying again soon, I expect."

They traded knowing looks. Tims waved him into the back room as he handed over the register to his assistant.

"Come, let us have a cup while we discuss our business."

Leaving Mouse and Anderssen to explore the store and chat with the lad at the till, they entered a cozy office. The Captain settled into a comfortable, threadbare armchair. Unlike the front, this room was cluttered with knick-knacks: bits of metal cogs and clockwork springs littered a bench in the corner, and Tims had to shift a mess of gears from the small table before setting down the tea service.

"I see you're still tinkering," said the Captain Duke, accepting his cup.

"Oh yes, I'll have to show you my latest gadget. A toy bear that can walk and sit and drink tea with my daughter. She's enraptured with the thing. She's named it Bobo and won't leave the house without it."

"And your wife?"

"Better. Much better. I've managed to advance a number of the designs you brought from the continent. Very useful, especially that ingenious device to toast bread. Her mood is much brighter now that she feels well enough to contribute, although she is still bound to the chair and must rest for much of the day. But she is much improved. Thank you. Thank you, Captain."

"Truly, I'm glad to hear it."

Tims gave him a watery smile before waving his troubles aside, "Now tell me of your travels, what caused your premature return?"

"We were ambushed by a contingent of soldiers. They have taken to guarding the Tradist ships now."

"By Victoria, how did you escape?"

"To be quite honest, I did not think we would. One of our new pilots was able to trick them into releasing us."

"The risks you take concern me, Captain, though we do appreciate your labours."

The Captain Duke nodded in appreciation, but was deep in thought as he sipped his tea.

"I was wondering…"

"Yes?"

"Have you heard any word of a shipment of gunpowder gone missing?"

Tims frowned, "Captain, what have you been into now?"

"What do you know?" The Captain Duke set down his cup.

"Nothing really. Only whispers. Something's afoot, but few will speak of it openly, even to speculate. I think—I think the Tradists are up to something. More than the usual. Something worse."

The Captain considered the news before continuing,

"What would you say if I told you we happened across a grain transport laden to the brim with gunpowder. Off the books. Even the airship's captain knew nothing of his patron."

Tims wiped his brow and sat back, "This does not bode well, Captain."

"No. Indeed it does not. This discovery, combined with our encounter with the soldiers–it cannot be mere coincidence. I know not the origins of the gunpowder, but I do suspect I have a traitor on my crew."

"If there is anything we can do for you…" Tims continued.

"Say the word, I know. In truth, I have come to give notice that we may need to adjust expectations for this year's haul. We will need to be more cautious after this incident."

"Yes, of course. I will tell the council to prepare for a leaner year. Have you been in touch with the Widow lately? She may have better information."

"She's a difficult one to get a hold of, but if my sources are correct she's expected back from the Americas soon."

"Good. We'll keep this small, only the closest of the alliance for now until we can determine the source."

The two men drank in silence, contemplating the turn of events. The 'liberated' goods were laundered through shopkeepers like Master Tims and sold below the posted price for the local farmers and villagers. Over the past decade he and Trick had developed a loyal network for the black market trades. Tims and the merchants were an essential part of his enterprise; they used the ill-gotten goods to supplement the overpriced stock provided by the Tradists. Without them, the stores could hardly turn a profit, and many of the essentials would be priced out of range for the common people. The Captain Duke had seen the effects of famine, and swore inwardly that he would do everything in his power to prevent such despondence.

Chapter 5: In which our heroine stops running

Clara looked over her purchases with pride. She had ordered two new gowns for wear about the town and a smart grey outfit with brass buckles that would work perfectly for navigating the port towns as part of their ruse. Mrs. Cottingham said she could find the perfect hat from the milliners down the street to complement the outfit as well. The dressmaker had a stock of clothes that were already fit to wear and only needed slight adjustments. Three new silk shirts and a set of fine black trousers were folded on the counter, along with heavy woolen stockings and a packet of underclothes wrapped discreetly in brown paper. But her favourite was an overskirt of deep purple that had struck her fancy. It was intended to be worn over a longer skirt, but she liked the way it was cut and draped to sit higher in front above the knees before angling lower in the back to cover one's derriere. It permitted some modesty while allowing her the ease of movement she had become accustomed to. Thankfully, Mrs. Cottingham was an advocate for the rational dress movement and greeted her transgressions with enthusiasm. The overskirt was a compromise between her past and present.

Mrs. Cottingham eagerly shared her latest book of patterns, including many of her own design that were geared towards practicality, in particular for the ladies who chose to cycle about town. Clara couldn't remember the last time she was actually excited about clothing, but it was the first time she truly had a say in the matter. She and Cat were enjoying a cup of tea with their new friend when the men returned.

"I trust you two have been well taken care of?" asked the Captain Duke. He looked concerned. Clara wondered at his business about town, but decided it best to leave the matter for now.

"Pickpocket," she stated instead, giving him an arch look over her tea.

The Captain let out a burst of laughter before reaching into his pocket to return her purse to her.

"An old trick. One I should probably teach you," he said. His smile had returned, along with its intriguing dimples. "Come, we will meet the others at the docks."

They took their leave of the dressmaker and hailed a mechanical cab to take them to the port. Clara helped to bundle Cat and Mouse into the carriage with their many packages, accepting the Captain's hand as he moved to assist her, in a comical, overstated performance of gentlemanly manners. He gave her fingers a gentle squeeze and winked when she met his eyes. She laughed at his antics and jovial mood, thinking nothing in the world could possibly spoil her happy mood. But then, catching a glimpse of the street behind him from the corner of her eye, she felt the blood drain from her face.

"Miss Clara? Miss Clara!"

Across the busy street, a man was straining to see them through the traffic. He gave a tentative wave. Clara's heart went cold as she feigned ignorance and ducked into the carriage as quickly as she could manage.

"Captain, hurry please. We must go."

At the urgency in her voice, the Captain Duke nodded and gave a quick order to the driver before joining them in the carriage. Anderssen swung up to sit on the back of the cab to watch for followers. Clara could feel their curious stares. She fixed her gaze on her hands, clasped tightly in her lap. They rode in silence for some time before she felt brave enough to see the Captain's reaction. He was still watching her. She looked down, cheeks burning.

"Clara?"

"I did not mean to spoil our outing."

"Who was that man?" he asked.

She was reluctant to reveal more, but she had put their venture at risk.

"An old acquaintance, the son of a family friend."

The Captain Duke considered this for a moment, "Did he get a clear view?"

"I can't be sure. Only for a moment I think," she said, wringing her hands together. Her chest was tight, and she felt a bubble of panic rising.

"He may doubt his perception. You said you were thought to be traveling the continent, did you not? When we found you?" He reached across the carriage to take her hand, "Do not torment yourself so. The Haven is safe. There are none here who would willingly reveal its location to a stranger. We take care of this town and it is in their interest to guard our secrets. Whatever the matter, you will be safe here."

Clara did her best to calm herself as they made their way back to the airship. The cooks were late in returning, and every additional moment spent at the docks caused her untold anxiety. When they were finally ready to depart, she sought her own company at the bow of the airship and was silent for the rest of the journey.

By the time they reached the Haven, Clara was determined not to allow her fear to discourage her. The life she thought she had left behind was catching up to her much sooner than she anticipated. Clara unpacked her purchases, then sat at the window of her room as she mulled over whether to share her secrets.

Clara was reasonably certain that her story would be safe with her new friends. Nessa would understand. She would never fault her for the choices she had made. She was far less sure about the judgement of the Captain Duke. He had ensured her safety without knowing her story in its entirety. What if he decided she was a liability to his crew and made her leave the Haven? Where would she go?

Clara sat for a long while, knees pressed to her chest as she stared through the glass at the forest below, until she heard a soft knock at the door that joined her room with Nessa's. Nessa entered, and at the sight of her friend, Clara's mind was made. She had to tell her.

"Nessa, you should be resting."

"I'm feeling much better. In fact, I hope you're feeling rested. We're beginning your training this afternoon."

"What? Nessa, I—"

"No complaints. Captain's orders. I'm not well enough to fight, and I do not enjoy the precariousness of our current situation. I need you to be able to defend yourself. Cat and Mouse will assist us. Are you ready?"

"Nessa, I need to tell you–" Clara said, before pausing.

"Yes?"

"Well…" Clara froze, she could not get the words unstuck.

Nessa leaned back against the wall.

"Cat said you had a bit of a fright this morning."

"I, well, it's not as though we were in danger, I just didn't expect to see…anyone."

"Clara, the world is much smaller than you would think. Believe me, I have seen a great deal of it. Whatever you are running from, it is inevitable that one day you will need to turn and face it. Face your fears, your past, whatever is holding you back. I've seen what happens to those who try to run forever, and it never ends well." Nessa walked over and placed her hands on Clara's shoulders with a look of determination, "Meanwhile, let me give you the tools you need to put up a good fight."

Clara hugged her friend, her own chest tight with emotion.

"Thank you."

Nessa smiled in return, "Good. Now, I sent Cat and Mouse ahead to the clearing; we'll meet them there."

They made their way down to the weapons room, where Nessa handed Clara a large bundle of padding. She nearly sank under the burden but soon found a better grip on the leather fastenings.

"We'll need to build your strength as well," Nessa said, laughing. They exited the room and Nessa led her into the surrounding forest.

Clara followed Nessa down a well-travelled path, only struggling slightly to carry her burden. Nessa's colour had greatly improved, although she did reach out to the trees for balance now and then. It was slow going, but their destination was not far. Clara could hear the sounds of wooden clacking nearly as soon as they entered the treeline. At first she assumed it to be some sort of bird or animal making the noise, but as they approached the clearing she could see that the noise came from Cat and Mouse, already sparring with wooden swords.

Nessa halted their progress and they watched as the two siblings parried and thrust like expert fencers. Cat had the advantage of height, but Mouse was untouchable as he tumbled and rolled beyond her reach, springing up behind her to launch a new offensive. Cat retreated until she neared the edge of the clearing, and Clara was certain that Mouse was about to win their match. Then, Cat changed direction, running towards a tree and using it to flip over her brother's head. She landed on both feet, holding her wooden sword at his neck. He pushed it away.

"Again," he said, assuming a fighting stance. He jumped at the sound of Nessa's applause.

"How on earth—" Clara began, but Nessa was already entering the clearing. "Well done," she called out. "But you need to stop falling for that trick, Mouse."

Cat beamed at the praise.

"Don't get cocky, he almost had you that time, Cat."

"Did not!"

"You need to learn to evade the attacks, like Mouse. You won't be taller than him forever and you cannot rely on your height for advantage in a real fight."

Mouse smiled and flipped Cat's sword out of her relaxed grip, tossing it towards them. Nessa caught it, but handed it to Clara instead.

"You'll be sparring with Clara today. Let's start with the basics."

Clara's concern over sparring with the two youths quickly vanished as she realized how thoroughly outmatched she was. They began with some simple stretches and exercises designed to increase one's energy. Cat and Mouse taught her how to move first, with Nessa offering her own corrections on form and posture from her position, seated and resting in the shade of a tree. Clara learned to roll without losing her sword and how to spin without becoming dizzy. She went through the drill again and again until her muscles were pained. Draw, roll, jump, spin, aim. Draw, roll, jump, spin, aim. Once her form was deemed satisfactory, she was ordered to repeat the feat a dozen times more. Finally, when she was certain she could do no more, they took a break to quench their thirst. Clara had never tasted water so fine and cool in all her life.

Then the real work began.

Clara picked up the sword and learned the proper grip after having it knocked from her hand a dozen times by little Mouse. At Nessa's instruction, the two children took turns teaching her thrusts and parries. They ran through the sequences slowly at first, until Clara could anticipate each move. Next, Cat and Mouse positioned themselves on opposite sides of Clara and she parried against the both of them, first blocking one attack, then turning to counter the other. Clara did not manage to win any of the matches, but Nessa said she was pleased with her progress regardless. They trained until a bell rang in the distance to summon them for the evening meal.

Clara dropped to the ground and lay flat on her back. "Finally! Can we eat now?"

"Do you surrender?" asked Mouse as he put his wooden sword to her throat.

Clara put a hand to her brow in mock submission, then grabbed the weapon and pulled the boy to the ground to tickle him.

"Stop! Stop! Noooo!" he squealed. Cat joined in to rescue her brother. After a few moments the three of them lay giggling on the grass with Nessa standing over them, hands on her hips.

"Well, if you have enough energy to play, you must have the strength to carry the equipment back. Come on you three. Time to sup."

Clara was bone-tired but thrilled with her progress. Her young instructors ran ahead while she and Nessa returned the sparring pads to the weapon room. She practically crawled up the stairs to wash and change, splashing water on her face and body. She took a deep breath and caught her reflection in the looking glass. Brown hair tangled in a messy braid, posture impeccable. But there was a light in her eyes that was not there before. Already she felt taller, stronger than before she joined the Captain Duke and his crew. Her mind was occupied with thoughts of how she would improve the next day in training, new moves to try, routines to memorize. As she hurried down the staircase to join the others, a figure stepped out at the landing, giving her a momentary fright.

"Oh, hello Miss Clara," said Robbie. He paused to wait for her to finish descending the staircase. She held her position, then, feeling rude, continued down to stand at his level.

"Hello, Robbie."

"May I accompany you to the hall?"

She ducked her head in the briefest curtsey. Her smile was more of a grimace, but the etiquette lessons of her instructor, Miss Ellington, were rather difficult to forget.

Robbie easily matched her pace with long strides. She stared straight ahead, barely acknowledging his presence though he prattled on about the Haven and its many features and amenities. As they turned down a corridor, he put out a hand to stop her. Clara recoiled from his touch, jumping back and raising her arm instinctively to block him.

"I beg your pardon, I did not mean to frighten you, Clara."

And with that, her etiquette lessons were forgotten.

"Frighten me? The very thought is offensive. Your familiarity is unwelcome."

Anger flashed in his eyes before he could arrange his features into a neutral expression. She saw the merest glimmer of the man behind the mask. She was well-acquainted with the many guises worn by those with less than noble intentions, the ways in which they used social graces to the advantage of their own nefarious purpose. He was a talented one. Resuming his act, Robbie stepped back and bowed.

"My apologies. I only wished to alert you to the location of a rather fine old portrait gallery in the next room." He paused before continuing, observing her defensive stance, "Clara, I am no traitor. I hope you will allow me to prove myself to you one day, or at least that you will hear my side of the issue with an open mind. I feel that we may have followed similar paths to this life, and I wish for you to know that you may find a friend and ally in me."

With that, he turned and continued down the hall. Clara narrowed her eyes. She did not trust him, but rudeness would not help the matter. She let out a breath of exasperation once he was out of sight and leaned against the wall. Despite her ravenous hunger, she was reluctant to continue to the dining hall. Unbidden, the thought popped into her mind that if she were home she could have the staff bring her meal to her rooms. She groaned and put a hand to her head. These memories were not useful.

"Clara? Are you unwell?"

She turned to find the Captain Duke staring at her from the end of the hall.

"What? Oh no, fine. I'm fine. Thank you."

He walked toward her, his concern showing itself in the line of his brow. He said nothing, but took her hand in his. Too tired to protest, she met his gaze and felt as though he could perceive her every worry.

"Tired, hungry, a bit homesick," she offered after a moment.

"Well, we can certainly rectify at least one of those. Shall we?"

The Captain tucked her hand into his arm and escorted her to the hall. His manners as a gentleman were impressive. Clara could see they were not the airs put on by some young men, but came from a place of genuine courtesy. They were a mark of his respect for others instead of an attempt to prove himself. Her curiosity about his background grew with every day she spent in his company.

Cat greeted Clara with a grin as she and the Captain entered together. She refused to blush, resolving to enjoy this moment of comfort and companionship as he led her to the head table to sit with Nessa and Trick. From the corner of her eye, she caught Robbie glaring at the two of them. She filled her plate with the fresh bread, roasted meat and thick, hearty stew. Still, there was something that unnerved her about that man. Clara hoped that whatever the Captain was planning could be acted upon soon. She put the matter from her head, as her appetite required immediate care. Soon, she thought, as she tucked into her meal, she would be ready to fight too.

Chapter 6: In which our hero makes no allies

"It's not like that at all. She's a nice lass. She saved us. You should have seen it, I was certain we were done for. And then up she came, dressed all lady-like and had them all—"

"But that's just it, isn't it? She's proven to be a mistress of deception and lies. Putting on airs and such – where did she come from anyhow? It's just too convenient she was able to get the grain and save the crew with nary a bullet fired. No one is that good. How do we know we can trust her?"

"The Captain Duke trusts her. And Trick. And Nessa. And Cat and Mouse, and by Victoria, those two can sniff out if someone's being dishonest."

"Well, the way I see it, Captain's judgement might be a bit clouded when it comes to her, if you know what I mean—hey now, don't get like that, I'm just saying she's a pretty one. Here he's blaming Robbie but what's more likely? That a good pilot is gone traitor to us all, or the Captain's been blinded by a pair of fine legs?"

"I will not stand to hear ill of Clara. She's a fine lass, like I said. A good, decent woman who has never done harm."

The past week had revealed more and more of Robbie's attempts to pick off members of the crew. Innocuous comments made during meal times, comments overheard during daily duties. And although the crew was kept busy with repairs to the ship, checking inventory and training, the extended break to allow Nessa to recover permitted a great deal of time for leisurely pursuits. They had delayed their departure for another week to allow her to rest. While he and Trick were busy checking the movement of Tradist cargo and examining the accounts, Robbie had ample opportunity to gather support. And his favoured strategy seemed to be casting doubt on Clara's intentions.

The two voices continued in their argument as the Captain Duke listened from around the corner, growing more furious by the second. Luk, one of Robbie's men, was arguing with Peg as she prepared food for the midday meal. The Captain was somewhat reassured that Clara had her own defenders among the crew, but Luk's arguments were disconcerting. Not that he believed a word of it. He knew Clara was genuine in her desire to be part of his crew. He had felt her tremble in his arms that day on the airship when she confronted the soldiers and saved them all. She lied to the lieutenant, yes, but her character was not deceitful. She was open and honest with him and his crew, showing reluctance only when pressed to reveal the details of her past life. But, if Robbie and his men intended to sow dissension in the ranks, they had found a grave weakness.

He listened until the two stopped their argument and waited until the sound of Luk's footsteps faded down the hall before slipping in to the kitchens. Peg was alone, preparing vegetables for something certain to be delicious. She didn't even pause in her rhythmic chopping as the Captain Duke approached.

"It's not looking good, sir."

"They are persisting with these tales of Clara's

duplicity?"

"Aye, Captain. That's the third to approach me in the last two days alone. All Robbie's closest. They seem to do his bidding, no knowledge of any plots. They are earnest in their defense of his virtue. All but that French one, Renault. And Maggie," Peg sniffed.

The Captain Duke wisely concealed a smirk. There were a number of Margarets on his crew, and at some point Maggie had cast aspersions over Peg's pet name. No blood was drawn over the affair, but the two had been at odds ever since. Thankfully, Madge remained above the conflict, preferring her potions and experiments over petty squabbles. *Never a good idea to anger those who prepare your food*, he thought, sneaking a small apple into his pocket. Peg winked in response, but then grew serious, setting down the knife and wiping her hands on her apron.

"Captain, is there anything to know? About Clara? I adore the girl, but if there's anything–anything–that could ease the others' minds…"

"Her secrets are her own."

"Aye, sir, but just think on it a moment. I don't appreciate all this sneaking about. Troubles should be faced out in the open. Robbie's up to something, of that I'm sure, but your own actions have played a part."

"My actions?" he knew his voice was angrier than warranted, but could not stand to have one of his most loyal crew doubting his leadership.

"Apologies, Captain. It's not my place."

"Please continue," he said icily.

"It's just the way of it Captain. Robbie's whispers only work because the crew is missing the old ways. You're more cautious now. It's not a bad trait in a captain, but they need tales to tell around the fire."

A kettle began to whistle on the stove. The Captain Duke grabbed the offending implement and slammed it onto the wooden counter to quiet it. Peg raised a brow. He let out a huff of breath.

"Peg, you know I appreciate your insights."

"Aye, Captain."

"I'll deal with Robbie. We'll be back in the skies before you know it."

The Captain Duke left the kitchens and walked through the halls of his home. He had built this, all of this, and would not see it destroyed or taken without a fight. He needed to deal with the matter of Robbie before the loyalties of the crew could be divided further. He felt as though he were poised on the edge of a blade, where any small thing could upset the delicate balance. It was an unpleasant sensation, manifested in the tightness of his chest and many restless nights.

In truth, he knew little of Clara's family or life. She had come over from the Isle of Wight, she had a brother named Archie, and had shown up in the cargo hold of a Tradist ship in a dishevelled ball gown, surrounded by gunpowder. The Captain Duke frowned as he considered how Clara's appearance would seem to the crew. It would certainly be easier if he or any of the others could vouch for her past. As far as he knew, she had confided in no one. Nessa would be the likeliest bet, or perhaps little Cat or Mouse, but certainly he would have heard something by now if it were so. He considered writing to his contacts on the Isle, but it chafed him to resort to such measures when the simplest solution was to gain her trust. Clara was an unknown element in a fractious situation. He needed certainties for his plans to work.

As he reached the door to his study, a voice called for him.

"Captain!"

Speak of the devil, he thought. She was hurrying down the hall toward him, face lit with an easy smile.

"Captain, I received a message from Mrs. Cottingham over the wireless. She says the clothing is ready for delivery. Are you free to discuss the scheme? I've done a great deal of research, but I do wish to review the details about the Tradist's manner and customs."

"Not now, Clara."

"Well, when? We would do well to take a few of the crew for a practice run of our plans. See how it works at one of the smaller ports first."

"I do not think they would take to it at the moment."

He watched as her smile was replaced with a frown.

"Why?"

"It's nothing for you to be concerned with. I have business to attend to, go train with Nessa." He opened the door to enter his study.

"Is that an order?"

He turned, "Does it need to be?"

"What is the matter with you?"

"Clara, I don't have time for this."

With bright eyes and a stern mouth, she crossed her arms, "Make time. You're acting oddly and I would like to know what I have done to offend you."

"Must every little thing involve you?"

Her face burned, but she still met his glare, "I was only trying to help."

"Is that why you're here? To help? To help by changing everything?"

"You said you liked the plan! It would decrease the risk to the crew."

"*You* are the greatest risk to my crew," he shouted.

Her silence hung heavy after the outburst.

"I know nothing about you, Clara. Who or what are you running from? Why the devil were you in a ball gown when you found us? You are all questions and no answers."

"I do not know what has sparked your mood but I will not stay to be abused by it. Pardon me for trying to assist where I am unwelcome," she said with an angry salute before turning on her heel.

The Captain Duke watched her skirts swish around the corner before slamming the door to his study. He ran his hand through his hair, angry at himself for losing his temper. He leaned his forehead against the wall and tried to take deeper breaths. First he had upset Peg, and now Clara too. He was not in a state to make allies today. He pounded a fist against the heavy door, and was surprised by a knock in response. He opened the door to discover Robbie on the other side.

"Good morning, Captain."

"What do you want, Robbie?"

"I came to give you an update on my findings. I think I know how our last raid went awry."

The Captain Duke glared at the man. He was not in a mood for excuses, but it had been a week since their return to the Haven. He opened the door further and allowed Robbie into his study.

Sitting in one of the armchairs, Robbie waited for him to take his seat behind the large desk. Instead, the Captain Duke stood before it, towering over his former officer.

"Well? What have you found?"

"Rumours, Captain. Just rumours. But interesting ones at that."

The Captain Duke waited in silence for Robbie to continue.

"When we returned to the Haven, I began to look into the origins of the gunpowder. I heard nothing back from our usual sources, as you are aware. But, I have a policy of staying in touch with characters of a particular repute, and one of them had a tidbit of useful information. I checked the logs, and the origins of the goods were quite clear."

"The Isle of Wight?"

"Yes. Clara's home it would seem. One of my contacts there is quite interested in her whereabouts, even more than the location of the gunpowder."

"What do you mean?"

"I'm just saying, the answers we seek may be found through the girl, not the goods. There have been a great many coincidences around this Clara. She was there for the raid, was she not? You said she rescued you all, a snip of a girl against a ship of soldiers."

The Captain Duke was outwardly calm, showing nothing of the tempest that raged within him. Even if he had his own questions about Clara's origins, she had been nothing but genuine, kind, and brave.

"Thank you, Robbie. I'll consider the matter," he said.

Robbie sat a moment longer, "Captain, she may be a spy."

"Enough," the Captain Duke barked, causing the other man to jump in his seat.

Regaining his composure, Robbie stood and made a short bow to the Captain before leaving the room, closing the door behind him.

The Captain Duke pushed his hair back, letting his breath out in a huff as he mulled over his options. Every mystery led to more secrets and he was no closer to the truth. He wished he could solve his problems with a good fight. He could teach Robbie a lesson. But the rumours would persist. Whispers could not be struck down as easily as the whisperer.

Swearing, the Captain kicked at nearby trunk. A number of packages fell out as the clasp broke, which did nothing to improve his dark mood. As he bent to retrieve them, the red binding of a book caught his eye. *The Press and the Public Service* by Grenville-Murray. It was the book Clara had given in exchange for her pilot's commission. He knelt and smoothed the pages. Another mystery. Why this book? He sat on the floor and skimmed through the opening pages, leaning against the upturned trunk. Slowly, his curiosity overwhelmed him and the solace of exploring a new book eased his temper. Taking a deep breath, he shook off the morning's trials, pulled the apple from his pocket and began to read.

Chapter 7: In which our heroine hears a song of the past

Clara stormed up the staircase and down a hallway, furious with herself for rising to the Captain Duke's provocation. How dare he presume to know her situation? How dare he demand her trust when he refused to reveal anything of his own history? And to infer, once again, that her reticence to delve into her past would endanger the crew. She had demonstrated her commitment and loyalty. She had saved them all from certain capture or casualty. *Twice.*

Training every morning with Nessa, sorting the accounts every afternoon with Trick, retiring every evening to the study to research a strategy for their scheme, Clara had never worked so hard or so happily in her life. She enjoyed the time spent together and she finally felt like a true member of the crew. To have him dismiss her hard work so casually—the very injustice of it stung.

Letting out a huff of frustration, Clara frowned as she reached the end of the hall. She looked upon the unfamiliar furnishings and realized she must have taken a wrong turn. She blamed the Captain for putting her in such a state as to become lost, another black mark on his reputation as far as she was concerned. She was turning about, trying to orient herself within the manor, when a faint melody caught her ear.

The sound was coming from a door on her left. Clara leaned against it, trying to determine its origin, and jumped back when the floorboard creaked under her weight. The melody stopped, and footsteps approached. She took a few steps back, embarrassed at being caught as an eavesdropper. But it was the smiling face of Trick who greeted her as he opened the door with a violin bow in one hand.

"Clara! How may I be of assistance?"

"My apologies, I did not mean to interrupt. I heard music."

"Yes, of course. Please, come in. I keep quarters in this wing so as not to disturb the others, but a keen ear is always welcome here."

Trick opened the door further and, to Clara's joy, revealed a parlour room filled with instruments of every shape and size. A grand golden harp reigned over a sunny corner, while one wall held an array of guitars and stringed instruments that framed an upright piano. An old bookshelf held the brass and many folios of sheet music, with a number of drums stacked neatly beside it. Trick's accordion held a place of honour on a small end table. The room was bright and well-appointed with comfortable furniture.

"Trick, it's beautiful," Clara said in awe. She took a few tentative steps into the room, amazed at the collection that surpassed any she had encountered or could ever have hoped to see. He beamed in appreciation and led her around the room to show his favourite pieces, pointing them out with his bow.

"I really ought to have invited you here earlier, only I never thought to do it."

"How did you come by so many?"

"Oh I liberated a few here and there from undeserving souls, to be sure. But truly our business has put me in a position to seek out rarities for my collection. See this? This one's called a sitar, I traded a kind Indian pilot one of my bodhráns for it. Beautifully crafted. Look at the way they've inlaid the wood. He strummed the instrument lightly, plucking out a delightful tune before returning it to its hook on the wall.

"What were you playing just now?"

"Oh, just a little ditty of my own making. It's nothing, really."

Sensing the performer's desire for encouragement, Clara goaded him into a performance, seating herself on one of the sofas. Trick retrieved his violin and closed his eyes, breathing in deeply as he drew the bow across the strings. Clara listened, breathless, as the melody pulled at her core. Soon, his warm tenor filled the room with a tale of home. He moved around as he played, lost to the music, weaving around the furniture and instruments in a familiar stride. Clara lost all track of time as she sat and listened to him play. The final notes lingered as he sat down across from her.

"Thank you," she said, when she had found her voice again. Clara put her hand over her heart, "Thank you, Trick."

"It was one of my first compositions once I grew tired of playing other men's songs. I still remember that night. I was terribly homesick."

"Homesick. Yes, I know that feeling. It's been nought but a month and yet it feels as though a lifetime has passed since I was on the Isle."

They sat in silence, deep in thought, until Trick broke the silence, "I won't inquire as to your own motivations for this life, Clara, as I suspect they may not yet be truly clear to even you. But I'll share mine with you, if you'll hear my story."

"I would be honoured, Trick."

He rose and carefully placed the violin and bow in its case, covering it with red silk before tucking it away.

"When I was a boy, my father could hardly tear me away from the piano in his shop. He was a successful businessman in our little town, selling spices and tea and dry goods from all over the world. Many of our neighbours lingered in their errands to hear me practice and take their refreshment at the little tables he had set up in the corner, and he would proudly tell all of his plans to send me to school on the continent for music.

"After the East India Trade Company was disbanded, a new group rose to take its place. I'm sure you know of this, but perhaps not the whole tale. For a brief time there was a good and fair exchange between the merchants and shops. But the Tradists had powerful ears in their service, and passed new laws in their own favour that pushed the smaller merchants out of business if they refused to join. This new monopoly—and trust that it is so, no matter what falsehoods they present to the world—it permitted the Tradists to set tariffs and prices out of reach for any who were not in their favour."

Trick rose and walked across the room, absent-mindedly picking up instruments and setting them down, "My father was one such unlucky man. They sold him low-rate goods and charged extra for the smallest convenience. His supplies dwindled as prices rose. His customers, even those who swore they would stand beside him, one by one they would no longer meet his eye as they passed him in the street." He brushed his fingers across the keys of the upright, "The piano was the last thing he sold."

"I remember the day they took the shop from him. He stood tall as he signed the papers. The three men wore fine red coats and shiny boots. The shop would go to one of their officers. He bought the piano for his daughters' amusement. We took our small bundles of clothing and left without looking back. As we walked down the street, my father took my hand – I was only nine years of age – and he leaned down to whisper in my ear: 'There will always be more, my boy. The music is inside you; they'll never take that from ye.'

"We found work with on a trading ship with one of the merchants who used to sell their goods to us. I took to the pilot's life well." Trick stood at the window, "The Tradists have their money and their tariffs and their rules. But they can never take the joys of flying through the air, nor the sweetness of music. Up there, all the indignities of life seem smaller."

"What happened to him? Your father," Clara asked.

"Oh, he found his luck again. He finally settled down with a lovely widow in the Scottish Highlands. She has grandbabies from her first husband that keep them well and occupied."

"Oh, that's lovely. So it was a happy story after all."

"We make our own fortunes, Clara. That's the lesson in it. You need not depend on others to seek your own happiness, although I suspect you are familiar with such ideas."

Clara met his eyes and smiled, "What of the Captain? However did you fall in with his sort?"

Trick let out a deep belly laugh, "I met him when he was just a scrap of a lad. Nought but 14 years on him, maybe 15. Big shock of fiery hair and the temper to match it. We were both commissioned to the same ship, see, and one night—" he cut off suddenly, looking behind her.

"Oh, do go on. Really, Trick. Tell me more about my fiery shock of hair."

Clara spun to see the Captain leaning against the doorjamb, hair tied back in a neat plait that defied Trick's description. In that moment, Trick's bright face rivalled the shade.

"I, uh, I do believe I have some business to attend to in the – in the storerooms. Yes. Urgent business. Must go straight away," said Trick, patting his pockets in a show of industry as he headed for the door. The Captain merely followed him with his eyes, not moving from his position as Trick squeezed past him. With a final wink at Clara, Trick ambled down the hall, whistling as he went.

Clara frowned, "He was only telling me a story. I asked him to." The casual amusement with which he regarded her was becoming rather annoying, particularly in light of their previous exchange.

"And you were curious about me?"

"No, I – he was telling me *his* story, you just happen to be part of it. Besides, it's not as though you are forthcoming on the subject.

"I am an open book, Clara," he said with a smile, crossing the room to sit on the edge of the sofa across from her. She shifted back in her seat. His long legs practically filled the space between them.

"First, I find I must apologize once again. I was in a cross mood, and you did not deserve it. Your secrets are your own, I had no right to pry into your affairs. I do trust you, Clara. And I hope that trust is shared." He leaned back and spread his hands wide, "Now, what stories is he telling about me?"

"You interrupted his story. How did you meet Trick?"

"We were part of the same crew."

"And?"

"And what?"

"Is that it?"

"You asked how we came to meet, that is an accurate account."

Clara narrowed her eyes, "Very well." She rose to leave, but the Captain laughed and reached out to stop her.

"Wait, I am sorry. If you wish, I will tell you this tale, but –" he took her hand with both of his and looked up into her eyes, "I do hope you will share more of yours with me one day."

Clara sat down and folded her hands in her lap. With a roguish grin, the Captain Duke began his story.

"Well, there were six crates of potatoes, and I thought no one was watching the cart…"

By the time the bell rang for the midday meal, they were both wiping tears from their eyes and clutching their ribs from laughter.

"All these years, he'll certainly never let you forget it."

"Oh I have a few tales to tell of his exploits, but perhaps we'll save those for another telling," he laughed. The Captain Duke cleared his throat, "Perhaps on our journey when we try this plot of yours."

Clara brightened, "Yes?"

"It's likely best if we keep it from the others for a little while; tell only those whose participation is essential. I need more time to judge the reaction from the other pilots. It's a… delicate situation at the moment."

"Yes. Yes, of course. I've almost finished examining the protocols. It will work, Captain. I promise you." She paused. "What changed your mind?"

"I did some reading." He let out a deep laugh, "In truth, I have faith in your enthusiasm for the idea. But dinner first, perhaps?" He extended an arm in a mock bow, which Clara accepted gracefully as they exited the room.

The Captain Duke squeezed her hand as he tucked it into his arm.

"Thank you," he said, stopping in the hallway and turning towards her.

"For what?"

"For reminding me why I chose this life."

He looked so earnest. Open. Happy. The reasons for his change of heart were unclear, but she was pleased by it nonetheless. Caught off guard by his sincerity, Clara finally gave into the urge to touch the bright strands bound in a plait that hung over his shoulder. She realised that he needed her companionship as much as she desired his own. An odd compulsion rose within her to be held by him. She wanted to feel his arms around her, to confide her every fear and aspiration, and to listen with rapture to his own. She took a breath and steadied herself. Instead, she gave his hair a playful tug and squeezed his arm in return.

"The pleasure is mine, Captain."

The two continued their progress down the hall, laughing all the way, neither of them aware of the angry eyes concealed behind a half-closed door that bore witness to their growing familiarity.

Chapter 8: In which our heroine befriends a spider

Clara was flushed with excitement. She had spent hours in the library over the last few days to refresh her knowledge of the current trade regulations between her training sessions with Cat and Mouse. She was more than sure of her knowledge; the deceit would be the hardest part. It was one thing to play at being a lady of refinement. She had extensive training in the matter, though she had thought it to be of little use until recently. And that ruse had the additional benefit of playing to type. The men on board that other ship wanted to believe in the fictitious damsel. As an Inspector, she would need to exude authority. She would need to show no uncertainty lest their targets see through the ruse. She wasn't entirely certain if she could pull it off, but she was more than up to the challenge.

Clara dressed herself in the new clothes sent over from the village and stared at her reflection in the mirror, running her hands over the fine grey coat. The clothing was perfectly suited to her purpose. Mrs. Cottingham was truly the master of her field. But something was off. The situation was not helped by the growing insecurity that marred her features. She tried to assume a look of confidence, but her efforts came off as haughty and childish. A knock at the door interrupted her affectation.

"Are you ready?" Nessa called, entering the room.

Clara met her friend with a look of desperation. "Nessa…"

"Oh come now. You'll do just fine. Here," she said as she picked up a brush. "Allow me." Quickly and without mercy, Nessa brushed out Clara's long dark hair and pulled it back into a tight French braid, tucking the end into a roll at the nape of her neck. The look was professional and austere. Intimidating.

"Better," said Clara, lifting her chin. "I wish you would come with us."

"Nonsense. I have much to do here to get things ship shape. I'm feeling much improved, I want everything to be ready to go as soon as the Captain gives his say-so. That means packing up the inventory and checking the books."

"Very well, but remember to rest."

"Yes, yes, and you remember to enjoy yourself. You are more than capable of pulling this off. Not that I remember your first attempt at playacting your way out of trouble, but the results speak to your talents."

Clara gave her friend a long hug before hurrying to the docks.

They took one of the smaller airships, just the Captain, Clara, and a few of his most trusted crewmembers. Only two were aware of their true intent: Anderssen and Peg. The rest believed that the Captain Duke had invited Clara to join him on a social invitation. They flew to Whitehaven, a port on the coast that had grown around the area's mines. It was not part of a major settlement and had no official Tradist post, so they hoped that they would find an easy time of it.

After they arrived, the Captain, Anderssen and Peg outfitted themselves in their new uniforms, deep blue jackets with brass buckles. The Captain Duke had his long, red hair tucked securely beneath a cap. For this venture, he would act as Clara's assistant. She stood at the helm of the airship before her team, black leggings tucked into tall leather boots. Her long, grey coat was fitted tight to her waist before flaring out in a new, peculiar fashion that mixed feminine and masculine styles.

The Captain Duke smiled and gave her a sharp salute, "Inspector Clarington, we are ready."

"Thank you. Gather the documents and prepare to disembark."

He laughed and she glared.

"Here, use these," he said, pulling a pouch from his satchel. It was a pair of spectacles.

"My eyesight is perfectly fine."

"As is mine," he said. "Try them."

Clara put them on. She could see no differently than before. She moved them up and down, but there was no change.

"Why on earth do you have a pair of false spectacles?"

"I have my reasons. Trust me when I say they greatly improve any deception."

"Well, thank you then."

"Are you ready?"

"Yes. Ready as I'll ever be." Clara adjusted the

spectacles on her nose and lifted her chin. She was rewarded by a slow grin from the Captain.

"Absolutely heartbreaking. They'll be eating from the palm of your hand."

She shooed him away and resumed her stern composure. It was time for action.

An hour later, Clara was leaning against the side of a tavern, kicking at pebbles. They still had found no likely candidate on which to practice their ruse. No merchant traders had docked this afternoon and Clara was growing frustrated. Anderssen and Mags had abandoned their jackets in the warm afternoon sun. Clara gently padded the perspiration from her brow. The Captain had left them to go and speak with the Portmaster, high above in a tower at the middle of the tallport stretching a hundred feet into the air.

Whitehaven's docks were spread out like a pinwheel, each of the three levels hosting airships of all shapes and sizes. Some were heavy transport ships, but none were currently loaded. Many were leisurecraft for the classes who could afford to travel the English coast. Postflyers zipped in and about, couriering their letters and parcels. The central tower contained an elevator for heavier goods, but many of the crates were conveyed to their destination by means of a mechanical track that twisted about the pillar. A staircase followed its path, the two twisting about the tower but never meeting. The new technology had left its mark on the town, with nearly every street filled with mechanized conveyances jostling for space. The coastal port had every manner of luxury good, with airships visiting from far off lands to the east and the west.

Clara was fanning herself in the shade when she spotted a ship passing overhead.

"Peg, what is that ship?"

"It's a trade ship, all right. From the Caribbean, by the looks of it."

"Excellent, it's exactly what we've been looking for. Now where is the Captain?"

"I don't see him. We should wait for his return."

"Oh, but this is the perfect opportunity! He must have seen its approach, surely he will come find us. Anderssen, you take the satchel. We're going to do this."

They buttoned their jackets and climbed up the broad circular staircase to the level above and walked briskly down the spoke to where the ship had docked. Clara took a deep breath to steady her nerves, and approached a tall woman who was standing near the gangway.

"Excuse me, pilot. I need to speak to your captain."

"Well, that would be me," she said, turning. Clara was momentarily stunned. The woman had coffee-coloured skin and black hair that was pulled back in neatly matted locks. Small ringlets curled around her face and her smile was bright and friendly. Clara had not anticipated a female captain, and she chided herself for holding to old prejudices.

"I beg your pardon, Captain. Allow me to introduce myself. I am Inspector Clarington."

"Captain Buchanan, at your service. What may I do for you, Inspector?"

"We have orders to collect samples of all tradable

goods," she said, handing over the formal document procured by the silent Anderssen. "The Association of Merchant Traders is performing quality inspections. We will only need to collect a small amount of your stock. You will be issued a receipt for the goods, of course."

Clara's heart raced as the woman examined her credentials with a furrowed brow. They had been carefully copied, she reassured herself. No one could possibly suspect them. After a long moment, the woman looked up with a hard stare.

"Well, the Association may rest assured that I only deal in stock of the highest quality. You may board."

Clara's heart leapt but she maintained her cool composure, "Thank you, Captain Buchanan."

She turned to shout orders to her crew while Clara turned to hand the documents back to Anderssen. Peg cleared her throat.

"Inspector Clarington. The Cap– your assistant has returned, Ma'am."

The Captain Duke was hurrying down the dock toward them. They paused to wait for him to catch up.

"Is everything in order, Inspector?" he asked as he neared.

"Certainly," she said with a smile. Then she watched his face freeze as Captain Buchanan turned to face them once more.

Something was terribly wrong. Clara tensed, preparing herself to fight or run as the situation required. She was stunned when Captain Buchanan began to laugh.

"Well, well. This is a new one," she said, staring at the Captain Duke.

He turned a shade paler than Clara thought was possible, "Marie, how are you?"

Clara narrowed her eyes and looked between the two captains.

"I think you all had better come aboard," said Captain Buchanan. Clara raised an eyebrow, but the Captain Duke gestured that they should follow.

"I presume that you are familiar with my 'assistant?'" asked Clara archly, once they were settled in a large office. The windows had been tinted against the glare of the sun. The cabin was cool despite the afternoon heat, dressed in bright colours. The three of them were sitting in woven chairs as one of the pilots brought in a cool, refreshing tea. Captain Buchanan sat with one ankle crossed over her knee. Clara's bearing was stiff and straight with ankles crossed in modesty. The Captain Duke shifted nervously in his seat between the two women. It seemed to Clara that Captain Buchanan was taking far too much enjoyment from the situation.

"Indeed I am familiar with the good Captain Duke. It is you who interests me. Not an inspector, I presume."

Clara was reluctant to break the ruse. But the Captain leaned back and smiled.

"This is Clara, a new pilot of mine. Please accept my apologies, Marie. We meant no disrespect."

"Very well, Olivier. But you will explain what in the

heavens you are up to this time."

Clara's eyebrows shot up and she snuck a sidelong glance. *Olivier*?

"Ah, I see you are still a man of many secrets."

"I prefer 'Captain.'"

"As do I, but what are formalities between old friends," she asked, showing her teeth.

Clara had the distinct sense that this was not a woman to trifle with and she had never been more curious about the Captain's mysterious past. Of course the first airship they met would be pirates. Still, she was determined to make an ally of this woman. She could be useful to the success of their endeavour.

"Please, the fault was mine, Captain Buchanan. If the Captain will permit me to explain, I would very much enjoy your feedback on our little ruse," she said with as much goodwill as she could muster.

"Drop the act. You smile like sugar but your eyes cut like steel," said Captain Buchanan. "I'll admit it, you nearly had me. It was a good attempt. Your first, I presume?"

"Yes."

"Why?"

The Captain Duke was silent. Clara glanced at him, and he gestured for her to continue.

"We... experienced some difficulty with a Tradist ship a few weeks ago. It was heavily armed. Far more than we were prepared to deal with. With some creative thinking, we managed to escape and secured a good amount of grain for our efforts. With these inspections, we may be able to collect the goods without as much risk to our crew."

Captain Buchanan was silent, sipping at the cool tea. The Captain Duke leaned forward.

"They nearly took Nessa."

"She's safe now," said Clara, seeing a flash of distress cross the other woman's face. "She suffered a concussion and some scrapes and bruises. But she is recovering."

"Nessa—What happened? How did you escape?"

"Clara dressed herself as a debutante and convinced the sergeant he had made a terrible mistake. And convinced him to throw a dozen sacks of grain into the bargain."

"I'm impressed. You must be an excellent liar."

Clara frowned. A stillness fell over the room. The tension was palpable as the woman looked her over. Clara sat straight in her chair and gave no indication of her racing heart.

Then, Captain Buchanan smiled. "I like you, Clara. But in the future, do not attempt any of your ruses on my ships." She rose and extended a hand. Clara stood to shake it.

"I am Marie Buchanan, Captain of *Ariadne.*"

A memory stirred in the back of Clara's mind, "Oh. From the newspapers?"

"From Haiti, actually," said Marie.

"Yes, of course. My apologies. You caused quite the stir here."

She laughed, "My late husband's family was not quite ready to embrace this new era. But they could not take my ships. Thierry and I were true partners in our trade."

Clara had heard of Marie Buchanan, but she was better known as the Black Widow, the slanderous moniker given to her by the papers nearly a decade ago that she had since claimed as her own. Those hounds always seemed to seek out the most salacious stories. Captain Buchanan's husband had been a wealthy landowner and merchant in the Caribbean, the last son of a prominent Marquis. His family did not approve of his choice of wife, and had engaged in a lengthy and sordid legal battle over his estate after his untimely death, issuing disparaging claims against Marie on the basis of her gender and race. Her victory against the regressive elements in the British colonies was also one of the first instances of the new reforms on women's property being successfully employed in a legal defense. She was also the first and greatest airship pilot to ever master the Atlantic trade winds.

"I am honoured to meet you, Captain Buchanan. I have heard tales of your crossings. Your skill as a pilot is legendary."

Marie smiled in appreciation, "Thierry always said he loved me for my wings, invisible to all but him. He told me if I married him he'd give me the skies. And that he did." She looked wistful for a moment before turning her attention to the Captain Duke. "He also taught me to hire the best for our crews. Name the day and you'll captain your own ship under my flag, Olivier."

"And here I thought you were after Nessa last time we met," he replied, unperturbed.

Clara thought for a moment that she detected a slight

blush on Captain Buchanan's cheek, but the woman merely raised an eyebrow in response.

"Good pilots are hard to come by and she is one of the best. Besides, I hear you're having enough trouble with your crew as it is."

The Captain Duke set down his tea firmly, "And what, exactly, have you heard."

"I received a message from Trick about a shipment of gunpowder. I sent my reply through the usual channel, but it was your officer, Robbie, who responded. He was evading my questions about your current location, and his line of inquiry seemed suspect. I had planned to make a stop at Keswick to check in with Tims about the situation."

"What did he say?"

"Robbie? He was asking about my contacts on the Isle of Wight."

Clara sat up straight, "The Isle? Whatever could he want there?" She sat back after the Captain Duke gestured for calm, but she could still feel her heart racing. Had he already discovered her identity?

"I do not know. I demanded to speak to you and he cut off the line. I'd watch out for that one if I were you. He's too ambitious with no good sense. But tell me how you came by this gunpowder and I'll tell you what I know."

The Captain Duke explained how they came by the shipment of gunpowder and their subsequent encounter with the soldiers during the next raid. Captain Buchanan listened carefully, asking questions here and there before sitting back and crossing her arms.

"I fear that our troubles are only just beginning," she said. "I've been receiving strange requests from the Tradists. And the Board has asked that I personally attend a meeting next month in London."

"And will you go?"

"They ask nicely, but you know as well as I that their requests are more like demands."

"That's the benefit of the black market—no one demands my presence. Besides, they need you. No one knows the Atlantic winds like you and your crews."

Marie smiled, "True, but their invitation has sparked my curiosity. I want to know what they're up to."

"I trust you'll keep us informed? I'll have Trick set up a new line on the wireless and send you the codes."

"Of course. And if you learn more about the origins of the gunpowder…"

"Naturally."

Their business concluded, they turned the discussion to her latest voyage from the Americas. Clara and the Captain Duke shared their plan. Captain Buchanan gave advice on the finer points, helping Clara to shape the scheme to suit the culture of the docks. She even had Clara practice her act, going through the motions for the better part of an hour before declaring them ready to proceed.

"It is one thing to pick off the Tradist ships in the skies, but another matter entirely to confront the captains in their ports. You have lost the advantage of the skies, but gained security in the likelihood that they will see you as less of a threat. You would do well to remember that, Clara. Use it to your advantage. I appreciate your plan to avoid bloodshed. It is a harder path for some, but a worthy one."

"Captain Buchanan, thank you. I truly appreciate your guidance."

Marie gave Clara a warm smile, and drew her into an embrace before stepping back and straightening her jacket, radiating the authority of her station. "Now, off with you. I'll send a few of my pilots along to spread word of this new inspection. Good luck, and send my blessings to Nessa," she finished with a wink.

Another ship had docked while they were occupied. Clara, the Captain Duke, Anderssen and Peg circled round to the spoke where it was tethered. The pilots were busy unloading onto the elevators in the central tower that carried the goods to the ground below. The men and women looked up at their approach, and one hurried to call out the captain. A short man emerged from the airship to greet them on the dock.

"Ah, you must be the Inspector. As you can see, everything is quite in order, Miss…"

"*Inspector* Clarington," she said with a severely arched brow, extending a hand. "I am certain there will be no trouble at all, Captain."

Anderssen loomed over them, producing the official-looking paperwork which the captain merely glanced at before gesturing to his ship.

"Welcome aboard," he said. "I'll gather the books."

By the end of the day, Clara had managed to try their ruse on three ships, collecting a mix of produce, textiles and fuel. They flew home over the rolling hills of the Lake District, thrilled with their success and discussed how they might expand their endeavour.

Chapter 9: In which our heroine duels with duality

Clara was quite pleased with herself. Since returning from their trip to Whitehaven, she had spent days poring through every text on the Tradists in the Captain Duke's extensive library, days combing through the ledgers with Trick to create a plan of action that had the potential to double their supplies. She had determined that the optimal strategy would be to hit the major ports in small groups of four and five. Clara, Nessa and Anderssen would be the 'inspectors,' with the Captain and his crew near enough to intervene if they met any trouble. They endeavoured to keep their scheme as innocuous as possible to avoid raising suspicion. Clara was certain that it would vastly improve the efficacy of the Captain's operations.

It was near to the end of their second week at the Haven and they were readying for departure. Soon it would be time to tell the rest of the pilots what they had in mind. Clara was preparing for an afternoon sparring session with Cat and Mouse before they finished packing the airships. She had just finished tying the bundle of padding together in the weapons room when she heard the door shut behind her.

"Hello, Clara."

Her grip tightened on the handle of the wooden sparring sword.

"Do you require assistance, Robbie?"

"As a matter of fact, I do."

She turned to face him, still holding the weapon.

"Oh come now. Surely there's no need for that. I only wish to talk. I have a matter of great importance to discuss with you."

"I'm afraid I'm otherwise engaged this afternoon. Perhaps another time."

"I'm afraid you'll want to hear what I have to say, Miss Whittington."

Clara's blood ran cold and the hairs on the back of her neck rose to attention. She could do nothing but stare at the man before her. He paused to smirk before continuing.

"Ah, yes. You see, I made a few inquiries. It was not difficult to find you. I had access to the ship's logs. I knew exactly which port you boarded at, the night of your departure. Imagine my surprise when I learned of your engagement. An Alexander Corring, I believe? My congratulations. Your fiancé is quite eager to know your whereabouts."

"You are mistaken. He is no longer my fiancé."

"Well there does seem to be some disagreement on that, but I'll allow you to sort that out yourselves. Now, you do have a choice in the matter…"

Clara kept her silence, tracking him with her eyes as he slinked about the room with a practiced carelessness. Finally, he turned.

"I need funds. You need my cooperation. Do you see

how our interests align?"

"So it is to be blackmail. Really, Robbie," she said, her voice dripping with derision.

"A partnership is what I'm proposing. To our mutual benefit."

"And if I disagree?"

"Then I'm afraid I will be obligated to alert him as to your location."

"To what purpose?"

"Ah, you underestimate him. He seems to have neglected to tell his creditors of your broken engagement. He's been spreading stories to any who will listen, and he is after your inheritance. In the absence of your family, there is no one to correct his lies."

"Nonsense."

"Is it now? As your fiancé he is entitled to concern himself with your affairs."

"Alexander Corring is *not* my fiancé."

"He appears to think he is. So does the rest of the town. As I hear it, in a fit of madness and grief, you ran out of your engagement party. He graciously agreed to postpone the wedding as you recuperate and recover your facilities. He is even prepared to be named as your guardian in the case that you maintain this state of madness. Think of how it would appear to the good people of Newport if they learned you had taken up with pirates? An heiress piratess? Really now."

Clara felt as though she had been waiting for something

like this to happen ever since she set foot on the Captain Duke's airship. She knew she could not conceal her identity forever, but to have it come out now, just when everything was coming along so well, it cut to her core. Her only option was to hope that her trust in the Captain Duke was not misplaced. But first, she had Robbie to contend with.

Two could play this game, and years of living in *society* had given Clara an abundance of experience with duplicity. Changing tactics, she arranged her features into an expression of tentative curiosity, allowing the tip of her wooden sword to dip slightly. Robbie beamed. *Amateur*, she thought.

"Tell me, what would this partnership entail? Why should I trust you over the Captain?"

"You've seen how slavish he is in his devotion to the 'cause.' If he learns of your true assets, he will covet your fortune for himself. Do you really believe that the Captain would be any different than your former fiancé in this matter? I, however, have no interest in controlling what you do with your funds. I merely wish to provide you with the opportunity to become a benefactor."

"And what would I be supporting, as your patron?"

"A much greater operation. Especially if you tell me everything you know about that gunpowder you came in with. I have sources who are very interested in supporting my endeavours. We could go anywhere, head for the silk routes where there are real riches to be gained. We could travel the world and I will double your fortune in a year. But tell me, what has your dear fiancé been up to, Clara?"

Clara stifled her reaction, the churning of her stomach and the sneer that threatened to mar her face. Instead, she demurred, playing up her birthright as a young lady. She lowered the sword, held awkwardly at an angle to the floor.

"I must say, it is a relief to be found out. It has been quite the adventure, but it is so tedious to conceal one's true self for such a time."

"I understand perfectly," he said, with a smile.

"You must also understand that I cannot agree to this matter before giving it some thought."

His smile turned to a grimace, "And you, I am sure, understand the consequences if you reveal our little arrangement to the others. I have my allies here, but we must wait for the optimal moment before proceeding. Timing is of great importance."

"And you will help me prevent Alexander's scheme to secure my inheritance?"

"I swear on my honour I will see to your safety if you agree to our partnership."

Just then, the door opened and Cat peeked in.

"Clara? Are you coming?" She looked at Robbie with suspicion.

Clara picked up the bundle of padding and tucked the wooden swords under her arm. She bowed her head in acknowledgement to Robbie, who winked as she passed him to exit the room.

As they walked to the woods, Cat turned to her with a questioning look, but Clara gave a small shake of her head. She waited until they reached the clearing where Mouse was waiting, making certain they had not been followed before sharing what had transpired.

"He knows my true name and threatened to reveal it to the Captain. I need to speak with him first, but I will be watched. Do either of you know a way to reach him without passing inside? We must not be observed by any; we do not know who Robbie's allies are."

"Well of course. We'll just climb up to the Bird's Nest."

"From the outside? Oh dear."

"We've done it a thousand times," said Mouse. "The Captain will understand."

Clara was still uncertain, but Cat stared hard into her eyes.

"You're one of us. You belong here, and the Captain knows it. Who you once were is not who you are now. He took us in and taught us that. And reminded us again and again until we knew it too. You can trust him. He always takes care of his pilots."

Clara took a deep breath. Her mind made up, she reached out to take the children's hands.

"I'm ready."

Chapter 10: In which our heroine speaks for herself

"Captain? I need to talk to you."

The Captain Duke was sitting at the desk in his personal chambers. He looked up in surprise as Clara entering from a passageway concealed by the paneling of the wall.

"Clara, what are you doing here?"

Clara crossed to sit in the armchair across from him, then rose again and paced the room. Even though she had planned an entire speech in her head, Clara had no idea where to start. She wished that Cat and Mouse were by her side, but they had been sent to fetch Trick and Nessa and she felt it important that the Captain hear her story first. He waited patiently, observing her distress, until she turned to face him once more. She took a deep breath and met his gaze.

"My name is Clara Whittington."

The Captain Duke was silent, but his eyebrows registered his shock.

"You may have heard… My father, you see. My family is—well, I'm sure that you know what transpired."

"Sit, Clara," he said, rising. He moved to a sideboard and poured a finger of good scotch into two glasses. She took her place in the armchair, hands shaking as she accepted the glass. The Captain pulled an ottoman closer and sat by her side.

"I am familiar with the name, but you will have to explain the particulars of your situation."

"Well, I— it's hard to begin."

"Let's start with your family, tell me about them." The Captain Duke reached forward and took her hand, "Tell me your story, Clara."

Clara took a shaky breath and sipped the fiery drink. The sensation helped to clear her mind, and she focused on the Captain's open expression. In that moment, her uncertainty cleared. This was a man she trusted. Calm now, she began to explain.

"My family is well known on the Isle of Wight. My father, James Whittington, was a trusted advisor of Princess Beatrice before he became ill. It was a long illness, very hard on my family. My mother, Elise, had a difficult time of it. She withdrew from her social obligations, content to care for Father and her gardens. After Father passed, nothing could cheer her. My brother, Archie, had to leave for school again soon, and she wanted to see me settled before she left for the continent to visit her sister in France.

"There was a young man. He had sought my affection ever since my debut. He was so supportive throughout Father's illness, visiting nearly every day and writing me letter after letter to raise my spirits. And he suggested that an engagement might improve my mother's mood. I was, to my eternal shame, besotted with the man. It was foolish, but the lure of stability after such devastation was such that I could not resist. And so I agreed to marry him."

The Captain Duke shifted in his seat at that, but urged her to continue.

"We were supposed to be in mourning. It had hardly been six months since Father passed. But my mother was never one to follow convention when it did not suit her, and she deemed it appropriate to have a small affair to announce the engagement. And, well…" she trailed off as her mind resisted the memory.

The Captain Duke waited in silence as she composed herself, for which Clara was immensely grateful. She could not handle any form of coddling at the moment. It had been the lowest moment of her life. But, she remembered, she might never have run away otherwise. The memory of that first day came to her, gazing through the portholes of an airship, wedged between the crates and the wall. A stowaway, imagining the endless possibilities before her.

The Captain Duke's silent support spoke volumes. Clara was stronger, physically and mentally, than the girl she was before. She had the freedom of the skies, the liberty to become herself. With a deep breath, Clara found her resolve, deciding there was nothing to regret about the events which led to this moment. They were part of the story that brought her here. Taking a sip of the scotch, she straightened her spine and looked the Captain in the eye.

"My fiancé was not an honourable man. The night before our engagement party, a woman carrying a swaddled babe presented herself at our door, inquiring about Alexander. He denied any knowledge of the woman, but my brother, Archie, followed him the next day as he slipped away and overheard their argument.

"You see, I received a rather generous inheritance from my father's estate. As of my 21st birthday last June, it is legally under my control. If I were to marry, it becomes the property of my husband." Clara could feel her cheeks growing bright with anger, "That was his plan all along. With my fortune, he would support her and their child. He was penniless, borrowing on the favour of creditors and the promise of marriage to an heiress. To me. Alexander had been anxious to wed since our courtship began, but any such thing was necessarily delayed by my father's illness.

"My brother told me of his scheme the night we were to announce the engagement. And I saw my life's course before my eyes, a loveless marriage and a penniless estate, forced to bear the scrutiny of the local ladies, growing old and bitter with no recourse.

"I was humiliated. Made to look a fool, before my family and my peers. I so narrowly escaped his trap, and I knew then that I would never be happy as part of that society. So I convinced my family to help me run away. It was crucial that I leave at once. I did not wish a confrontation that could result in Archie being forced to duel over my honour. I love him dearly, but he is a scholar, not a fighter, and I would not put it past Alexander to force my hand with the threat of violence. Mother was not pleased by the idea, but agreed to travel to visit her sister in Europe as planned and pretend I had joined her so that I would have some reprieve. Our neighbours would be informed that I was too distraught to go through with the engagement. I thought that would be the end of it. Clearly I underestimated his tenacity."

"Well. That explains the dress at least. But this Alexander, he believes you are still engaged?"

"Yes. Apparently he has disregarded the note I sent to him. Mother will be furious when she returns. It is quite inconvenient."

“I believe it may be time to pay him a visit,” the Captain said with a murderous look.

Clara couldn’t help the smile that crossed her face at the thought of a confrontation between Alexander and the Captain Duke.

“Not now, we have other matters to attend to. Leave my former fiancé to me. I have a few ideas.”

“As you wish. Clara, I do not know what has prompted your confidence in me, but I assure you, you have my support and that of my crew in whatever you choose.”

Clara stared for a moment before the realization came to her.

“Oh! Drat. It was Robbie? Did I not tell you? He tried to blackmail me, and he’s planning a mutiny.”

“What?” he roared.

Before Clara could say another word, the Captain Duke stormed to the door and opened it. He prepared to shout for Trick and Nessa, but they were already waiting, along with Cat and Mouse. Ignoring his furious look, Cat skipped into the room.

“Well I suppose she’s told you then. We gathered the officers, Captain. Figured you might want to chat before dinner.”

With a look of exasperation, he gestured the rest of the company into the room to take seats around the small space.

Clara told them of her interaction with Robbie, and briefly recounted her own story. Then she sat back and listened as the others argued over what to do with the information. The possible connection between Robbie, Alexander and the gunpowder was of particular concern. It was clear that Robbie was planning to act soon if he was willing to risk reaching out to her. Trick shared what he had gathered among the crew: who was divided in their loyalties, and who remained firm in their support for the Captain Duke. They spoke late into the afternoon before dispersing to engage those who could be trusted in their plan. At dinner, they were to come armed.

Chapter 11: In which our hero attempts a diplomatic resolution

The Captain Duke's mind was racing as he paced about his study. His blood ran cold at the thought of who might stay and who would go if offered the chance to follow Robbie. All these years without a mutiny, and to have it come at the hands of one of his most trusted officers stung more than he would ever admit to Trick or Nessa. He refused to allow Robbie's deceit to fester any longer. If there was to be a split, it would be tonight.

A knock pulled him from his reverie. Trick entered, closing the heavy door behind him. The two men exchanged a significant look before the Captain resumed his pacing.

Trick waited before speaking, "Are you certain you want to do this tonight? We could give it a day or two, gather more information."

The Captain Duke stopped before the window, gazing out at the scene before him. It was the golden hour. The sun cast the island in warm tones as it began its descent towards the horizon. The tranquility of the moment did nothing to ease his mind. But, taking a deep breath, he thought of how he had carved this place into his home. He thought of the decade or so spent fighting, stealing, and flying to create his empire. And he was tired. So very tired of it all.

"Yes. Tonight," he said. Trick joined him to stare out at

the scene in a reverent silence for a long time until Nessa called for them. The Captain Duke checked his pistols and tucked extra ammunition into his coat. Trick placed a hand on his shoulder.

"We will stand with you, Captain."

The shadow of a grin passed over his face for the briefest of moments, "I'm ready."

The dining hall was as boisterous as always, with pilots filing in from their duties. The excitement was palpable; preparations for their departure were almost complete, and the women and men were happy to enjoy a final meal from the Haven's abundant kitchens before returning to the skies. The Captain Duke paused at the entrance, making note of those who had gathered with Robbie in the corner furthest from the head table where Clara and Anderssen sat, deep in conversation. There was no sign of Cat and Mouse and the Captain hoped they would follow his orders to stay safely away. Stone-faced, he walked through the room, flanked by a grim Nessa and Trick. Instead of sitting, he stood before the long table, facing the assembled pilots. A hush fell across the room as they turned their attention to the front of the room. He waited, allowing the silence to fill the space before continuing

"Tomorrow, we fly."

Cheers erupted from the tables, and the Captain Duke waited out the round of applause.

"It has come to my attention, however, that there may be some disagreement about the methods we employ to pursue our objective."

The crowd stilled.

"In truth, the nature of our trade is changing. The world is not as large as it once was. We have adapted to this new order of things, and to continue we may yet again need to change our ways."

He took a step forward, clasping his hands behind his back. The hum of anxiety was palpable as he scanned their faces.

"I've been working to devise a new strategy. A more prudent way to conduct our 'business' with the Tradists," he smirked, and was rewarded with a few laughs from his crew.

"But, before we continue, I need to know who will stand with me. Many of you have fought by my side for years. You have earned my respect and my gratitude. We have carved our place here with blood and swords and Tradist tears. The winds carry whispers of our deeds to every corner of the globe. Come with me, and I will give you the skies. But—" he paused, "But if our way is not to your liking, now is the time to go."

He scanned the faces before him. He watched as eyes flicked towards Robbie, who sat silent, staring straight ahead, toying with his fork. The Captain Duke stared back, arms crossed. He did not wish to think on the actions that must be taken if Robbie refused the opportunity before him. The silence stretched on into minutes.

At long last, Robbie acknowledged the glances in his direction.

"Bloody hell, don't pretend as though you're buying the man's lies."

A shiver ran through the room.

Robbie stood, pointing a finger at the Captain Duke, "You sit there all high and mighty, talking of different ways. The truth is you've lost your appetite for this life. Admit it." He turned to the assembled pirates, "You think he could have built this without us? He looks down on us and our taste for violence, but it's fine and well for him to profit from it."

Robbie paced through the tables before stopping in the centre of the room, "The Captain *Duke*," he sneered. "You have forgotten your place. You fight battles with your reputation to avoid bloodshed. At the first sign of a real fight, you flee back to your Haven to lick your wounds."

"And where were you, Robbie Codswaddle?"

"What do you mean where was I? Oh-ho-ho, you see how he twists my words?"

"Where were you when we fought against the Tradist guards? Here, in our Haven, deep in your cups after sending our pilots into a trap on bad information. A captain protects his crew. Your incompetence nearly cost Nessa her life. The difference, Robbie, is that I value life over lifestyle. If your wish is to steal and drink all the day long, you are free to do so. But you will not do it here. You speak of me forgetting my place? You ignore my purpose. Every last one of us has been affected by the Tradists in some way. We have seen the effect of their work. We take and we give; we are responsible for our actions, but our actions have the consequence of bettering the livelihood of others. I admit, I am not a man of high morals, but I am more than a greedy thief who whines at having to share his bounty."

"A thief? Your true feelings at last. You see how he perceives us? Will you stand for such words?"

The Captain Duke held his breath. No one spoke in Robbie's favour, but there were some who would no longer meet his eyes.

"You were right about one thing. I had lost my way. I doubted our enterprise and questioned its worth. But I see it now more clearly than ever." The Captain spread out his arms, "Friends, we need not be divided. Stand with me and together we will fight to bring the Tradists to their knees before the people they have wronged."

"Your head is in the clouds, Captain. You think our little skirmishes make a difference? The Tradists run the damned world," said Robbie.

"You think our battles mean nothing? Tell that to the people of Keswick. Tell that to every man, woman and child who has avoided starvation because of the food we steal. How many have clothed themselves with our wool? How many kept their farms with the seeds we share? The small things count. They grow and amass into bigger things. That's how change happens."

Robbie laughed, "It is not enough. The decent folk have made their choice to be complacent. Maybe once they are starving they will learn to fight like the rest of us."

The Captain Duke was shaking with fury. He fought for composure and allowed the man's words to carry through the hall, echoed by the murmurs of the pilots, many of whom had watched loved ones go hungry in those first bitter years of Tradist control.

Nessa came to stand beside him, whispering under her breath, "Say the word and I'll put a bullet through that tongue of his."

The Captain Duke was dangerously tempted by her

proposition. But he still believed a diplomatic resolution was achievable. It was the safest route, and he would not treat the lives of his crew so casually. Still, he brushed his coat back to stand with hands on hips, fingers twitching toward his pistols.

"Robbie, you are banished from my crew. Leave, and never return. All who wish to go may follow him without harm. But, if you ever cross us again, I will slit your throats myself."

A stunned silence fell over the room. After a moment, Maggie stood and walked over to stand behind Robbie. A half dozen others joined them. Not as many as the Captain Duke had thought might go, but enough to sear his heart. He nodded at Anderssen to lead them out. The small group turned to follow Robbie, leaving the Haven forever.

Chapter 12: In which our pilots pass the point of no return

For a moment, Clara felt as though she could breathe again. Robbie and the pilots who chose to go with him were leaving. With narrowed eyes, the assembled pilots watched as they were led from the room. It happened so quickly, she almost missed it.

Anderssen doubled over, clutching at his chest.

Robbie turned and raised his pistol towards her.

A great force slammed into her, pushing her aside as a shot rang out.

Clara felt the Captain's body over hers. She felt his tension as he shouted orders to his crew. With a quick glance to see that she was unharmed, he leapt to his feet, pistols drawn.

Chaos. That was the only description she registered as former allies fought each other.

Clara hid behind a table as the battle moved into the foyer, her heart beating so hard she thought it might burst from her ribcage. Pistols. Her pistols. They were strapped around her waist as usual. She checked to make sure they were loaded and peeked around the side. She could see Anderssen's boots lying prone, and blood pooling on the floor. Staying low she made her way over to him.

His eyes were barely fluttering. His breaths came in short, painful gasps. Clara found the knife wound and applied pressure to halt the bleeding. Shrugging off her coat one arm at a time, she rolled it and placed it beneath his head. She looked for something to bind the wound but was stopped by a gentle hand on her wrist. Anderssen opened his eyes and looked into her own.

"You're going to be fine. One of the nurses will come soon. We'll get help."

Anderssen tightened his grip on her hand for the briefest moment. Clara felt her own heart grow cold and she squeezed his hand back as hard as she could. She leaned down to whisper words of comfort, as though she could shield him from the coming end. He smiled at her as the life left his eyes.

Clara clutched his body to her chest. The tears rolled down her cheeks of their own volition. He was a good man, a kind one. A man who did not deserve to die in a pool of blood on the dining hall floor. Hand shaking, she closed his eyes against the world. Laying his head down on the floor, she shook out her jacket and covered him with it. A burning fury was swelling up in her core.

Checking her pistols once more, she wiped away her tears, leaving great smears of blood across her face. Then she ran to join the battle.

Chapter 13: In which our hero faces an unthinkable prospect

The Captain Duke used the staircase for cover as he shot at the traitors down the hall. As soon as his pistols were unloaded, he ducked behind the wall so Trick could take his place. He was glad they had taken the precaution of carrying extra bullets, despite hoping for a different end to their trouble. But he knew that they would run out eventually.

"What do you think, Trick?" he asked as the other man ducked down again. A near shot tore into the plaster of the wall across from them.

"They'll go for the ships as soon as Robbie gets his act together. We need to get there first."

"The window then. I'll cover you."

He waited while Trick reloaded his pistols and made sure his sword was securely fastened around his waist. The Captain Duke took a deep breath and steadied himself, then with a curt nod to his first mate, he rose and began to shoot through the banister.

Trick somersaulted to the window and shot the latch open. He lifted the heavy pane and put one leg through the frame, aiming his pistol down the hall as the Captain crossed to the window, still firing. The Captain took one last shot as he jumped out and held the frame for his friend. He nearly let go when a shot grazed the wood by his fingers, but Trick rolled out to leap to the ground, and they ran to the corner of the building.

Trick collapsed, clutching his arm and swearing.

"Bastards! Bloody goons born under a halfwit moon! Damn them to seven hells!"

"Show me."

"Go, go. I'll bind it and find somewhere safe. Here, take an extra pistol with you."

The Captain Duke tore off a piece of his own shirt and pressed it to his friend's arm. "Be safe," he said, and ran for the airship docks.

What greeted him there was possibly the most frightening sight he had ever seen.

Robbie and three of his men had already made their way to the docks and were shouting as they ran up the staircases and climbed the ropes. High above, Cat was swinging across from ship to ship, cutting their tethers and sending them adrift. Mouse had already taken the helm of the Captain Duke's ship and was shouting for her to hurry when one of Robbie's men reached the landing and shot at her before she could untie the final vessel. Instead, Cat ran for the other end of the port, strapping on a glider.

The Captain Duke charged into the clearing, yelling for Robbie to face him like a man, but he was too late. Robbie reached the top of the stair and aimed his pistol at the girl.

"Now, Catherine, dear. Do tell your brother to come back down like a good boy."

With a fierce look, Cat stepped back and plunged toward the ground, banking against the wind and gliding up to join her brother on the ship already loaded with all their supplies. Robbie took one shot that missed, and then scrambled to launch the other airship with the help of the three men with him, yelling incoherent orders.

The Captain Duke watched her fly from the edge of the clearing, waiting until Cat was safely aboard his airship. He signalled to the children to head for the town, heart bursting with pride as Nessa joined him.

"They've cleared out, Captain. Kathy and Luk escaped on the boat, Jimmy and Renault surrendered. Peg and Mags are having a bit of a face off, but those are the last four."

"He won't get far with that ship. The others are faster."

Frantic waving from Cat and Mouse caught his attention. They pointed at the port and shouted something inaudible. They were too far to hear. The Captain Duke saw Robbie and his men strap on gliders as they launched the airship to fly south over the Haven.

The Captain Duke jumped as Nessa grabbed his arm.

"Captain! Which ship is that?"

He turned to her, "It's just a merchant ship, the one we stole when we found Clara—"

The blood drained from their faces as they turned to race back through the trees. The Captain Duke's heart was pounding, filled with dread, even as his mind turned away in denial. It couldn't possibly come to this. Robbie could not be capable of such a thing. Still, he tore through the woods to reach the Haven as the airship above closed the distance between them.

"RUN!" he shouted to his crew as soon as the first pilots came into sight. He sent Nessa around the other side to find Trick as he ran into the house,

"Run! Warn the others! Get to the water!"

The Captain Duke ran from room to room, sounding the alarm. Pilots rushed to help the injured escape, friend and traitor alike. He found Anderssen's body in the dining hall, covered in Clara's jacket. *Clara*!

Nessa called for him from the back, "Captain! Now, come now! You must."

"Clara? Clara!" The Captain Duke shouted, racing for the stairs.

He was grabbed forcefully from behind as Nessa pulled him to the door,

"Don't make me knock you senseless, you fool. It's time to go. She's outside, I'm sure of it."

"Did everyone get out?"

"There's no time to check, go, now!"

They burst from the house and ran for the shore. He didn't look back at his home. He couldn't. The airship had been set alight above them. He could hear the pop of bursting portholes and see the orange glow inside the hold. Any second now, the gunpowder within would catch and burn. The blazing vessel was aimed straight at the Haven.

Chapter 14: In which our heroine reaches the Haven's end

Clara found the others fighting in the hall. Half of the traitors were missing, but she spared them little thought as a bullet whizzed past to embed itself in the centre of a painting beside her. She crouched behind a pillar, timing her shots with her fellow pilots. There was no way the traitors could overpower the Captain Duke's crew; the numbers were against them. Clara figured this must be a delay while Robbie escaped. They needed to get out, but the quickest way out was the door that stood beyond their more immediate foes. She counted the shots in her head and signalled to Peg to follow her lead.

She heard the click on an empty chamber and jumped out in the interval as the mutineers switched places to reload. The smear of Anderssen's blood on Clara's face lent her the ferocity to match her yell as she barrelled down the hall. She launched herself into the air with the help of an overturned chair, spinning as Cat had taught her, landing on both feet with pistols pointed at the two men who looked, frankly, in some degree of shock at the sight of her.

"Surrender."

Renault twitched as though to fire, but Peg kicked the gun from his hand as she joined her.

"Surrender or die, you cowards. Clara may not be

willing, but you know I'll shoot ye."

The two men quickly allowed their hands to be bound at their backs.

"Where are the others?" Clara asked.

"Outside," she responded. "Is that?—" Peg reached out to touch the blood on Clara's face.

"Anderssen."

Peg's eyes grew cold. She shouted for Cook to take the men away, then gestured to Clara to follow her as they chased the sound of the skirmish outside.

Nessa was leading the chase as three pilots ran for the old boat tied up at the shore. Maggie held them off as the other two, Kathy and Luk, fumbled with the knotted ropes.

"Nessa! Cook is holding two who surrendered, where are the others?"

"That's most of them accounted for. I've half a mind to let these three go. Robbie isn't here. The two of you stay here and watch to see if he joins them, I'm going to check the port."

Nessa ran into the trees as Clara took up position in the cover of an outcropping of rock. It was a standoff, each side waiting for the other to make a move. Peg and Maggie traded barbs, but long moments passed while she crouched, ready for action. Still, she was not prepared for what happened next.

She saw Maggie's mouth drop in shock before she turned and ran for the boat. Clara looked around for any sign of Robbie, but it looked as though the three were abandoning their co-conspirators. Then she heard the shouts and the crackle and pop of fire.

Clara turned to look back at the Haven, bathed now in an odd glow, though the sun had already sunk beyond the distant hills. Curious, she began to walk towards the clearing.

It was surreal. The woods seemed to still around her as she stood frozen at the sight. She swore she could see the very porthole on which she had rested her cheek just weeks ago, lit by flames within as the airship, magnificent in its horror, steered towards the Haven. The flames danced along the decks and the ropes to the balloon that held it aloft, reflected in the grand windows of the manor. The ropes snapped and the vessel sank, hitting one of the northern gables with a crunch that echoed through the trees. And then, all hell broke loose.

Clara could not remember the explosion. When she opened her eyes, the world was on fire and her ears rang with a piercing whistle. There was metal embedded in the trees around her. She had fallen amid rocks that must have shielded her. But in her confusion, she could smell the forest burning around her, and scrambled to get to the water. She found Peg, collapsed on the shore. Her face was bloodied, but her breath was steady. Clara arranged her as comfortably as she could before standing to find help. She shook uncontrollably from head to toe as she ran along the shore.

In the sky, another strange sight. A burning glider sweeping erratically through the air as the pilot made a futile effort to snuff out the flames. Clara paused to watch its dizzying descent as it narrowly missed the treeline and crashed into the shallow beach. As the pilot extricated himself from the wreckage and stood, backing away from the flames, something clicked in her mind to clear the fog.

Hand trembling, she raised her pistol. He was no more than a dozen steps away when Robbie turned and saw her.

"Clara. Clara, wait."

Clara could not say a word. Her hand was shaking badly; she tried to steady it with both. This man had killed people she cared for. He had destroyed the Haven, torn apart the crew she had grown to know and adore. And still she could not bring herself to pull the trigger. Clara knew how to aim and how to shoot, but there was no training that could prepare her to take someone's life. Slowly, Clara lowered her arms.

It may have only been seconds that passed, but it felt like an eternity as she watched his fear fade, replaced with relief, and then…contempt.

Robbie turned and ran into the waves without looking back, swimming out to the call of his fellow traitors in their waiting boat, disappearing into the gathering darkness. Clara fell to her knees and screamed, tossing her pistol aside.

"Clara!"

She turned to see the Captain Duke at the treeline. He ran to her, kneeling down to touch her face, her hands.

"You're bleeding."

"Not mine, I think."

Clara looked into his eyes and realized what she needed. She leaned forward and kissed him. Once she started, she could not stop. The Captain Duke pulled her to him, clutching her as though he held to life itself. She ran her fingers through his fiery hair, pulling him closer. Clara wanted this, needed this. He wrapped her in his arms and pressed his body against her own as he deepened the kiss. He made her feel alive, he made her feel powerful. Kissing him made the world feel right again, and she never wanted to stop. But just as soon as the feelings washed over her, the reality of their situation struck. She pulled away.

"I couldn't do it, I couldn't."

"What—couldn't what? Clara—" the Captain Duke tucked her hair behind her ear, still holding her close.

"I saw him. Robbie. He was here, but I couldn't shoot." The tears began to roll down her cheeks. Tears for Anderssen. Tears for Peg. Tears for the Haven and the way things were before. Nothing would be the same now; the world had shifted in some immutable way.

The Captain Duke moved to sit on the rocky shore so he could wrap his arms around her. They faced the water, backs solidly to the wreckage behind them. He stroked her hair, whispering that all would be well as she sobbed into his shoulder. They sat like that for a long moment before she finally dried her eyes. She clasped his hands between hers as she sat, rather indecently, between his knees, leaning back against his chest. She stared a thousand yards into the darkness, seeing nothing as her mind tumbled in all directions. But then…

"Captain, look!"

The Captain's ship was returning, and it wasn't alone. An entire fleet followed: every able vessel of Keswick. Clara and the Captain Duke watched in silence as the airships sailed over them towards the Haven, dumping water onto the blaze. Clara stood and pulled her captain to his feet. He only stared at the vision before them, overcome. Clara squeezed his hand in response. It was her turn to comfort him as they watched those who he had shielded from harm for all these years return the favour. Slowly, hand-in-hand, they made their way back towards the clearing to join the cheering pilots.

Stay tuned for Book 3!

Tales of the Captain Duke:

A Gentleman and a Scholar

rebeccadiem.com

Archibald Whittington
c/o Lovelace University
Reading

~~My dearest brother,~~

~~I hope my letter finds you well. How is the weather in Reading? I hear it's delightful this time of year.~~

~~Dear Archie,~~

~~Apologies for the delay in writing you, I have joined a band of airship pirates.~~

~~Archie,~~

~~I don't know where to begin. I was found by pirates in a shipment of gunpowder, caught up in a traitor's plot, and now the Haven is destroyed and there was a battle and I can fight now but I could not shoot and~~ –

Dear brother,

I need your help. Please come.

– Clara

Bonus: In Which Our Invalid Plots Her Revenge

A parallel to Chapter 4 & 5 of From Haven to Hell (Tales of the Captain Duke #2), as featured in the July 2015 edition of Airmail.

Nessa waited until the sound of the *Zephyr's* engines had faded into the distance before slipping out of her room. Too many days spent trapped in her sickbed, she was not going to waste this chance at a bit of freedom while the Captain Duke was away in town with Clara. Nessa did hope that the two of them would settle their differences and get on with things already, and would certainly do her part to push the two of them along, but in truth she wanted a morning away from her caretakers' watchful eyes.

Her advantage lay in the expectation that she was too weak to cause trouble. The expectations of the fairer sex had served her well in many battles to undermine her opponents. And in truth, though the throbbing headache pounding in her brain had subsided to tolerable levels, Nessa was quite aware that her current state of limited usefulness was likely to continue for some time. Assessing her options for revenge, she set out to address her most immediate target: Robbie.

Nessa knew the Haven nearly as well as Cat and Mouse. Careful not to upset the squeaky hinges of the concealed panel, she entered an old servants' stair and snuck into a hall formally used by household staff to move between the rooms unseen. She crept along the narrow passageway until she heard his voice. Robbie was in the parlour, enjoying a mid-morning game of darts with Renault while the simpering Maggie looked on. They were discussing trivial matters, but Nessa made herself comfortable, peeking through a small vent. Soon, her patience was rewarded.

Peg entered the room, apron smudged from her work in the kitchens,

"What do we have here? Gadabouts, the lot of you. Don't you have duties to attend to?"

Maggie rolled her eyes dramatically and jumped down from her perch on the windowsill, "Who put you in charge? We're pilots, not cooks. Do you see any flying to be done?"

"Ladies, ladies," Robbie interrupted, moving between the two women. "There's plenty of leisure to go around. Join us for a match, Peg, you play a good game if I recall."

"You think you can lay low while this storm blows over? You are dead wrong, Robbie. If I were you I'd be worrying less about my aim and more about Nessa's once she's up again. Hell hath no fury…"

Nessa smiled from her hiding place, but remained silent as Trick entered the room behind them.

"There you are. Peg, the Captain should be back ere long and I want to go over some figures with you for the restock. It could be a week or more before we're back in the skies."

"Right away, sir," answered Peg, shooting Robbie a dark look before heading for the door.

Maggie snickered, "Yes, back to the kitchens with you."

Nessa had to stifle her laughter at the severe look on Trick's face as he turned back to the three delinquents.

"Maggie, we accumulated a great deal of excrement on the canvasses since the last rainstorm. How fortunate that we're grounded this week so you'll have the opportunity to clean them. How kind of you to volunteer. Robbie, Renault, of course you may assist."

With that, Peg and Trick left the parlour.

Robbie swore and flung a dart at the board, missing it entirely.

Renault was too busy being horrified to notice, "Ce n'est pas juste! Those canvasses are filthy."

"Listen to him, grounded for a week or more he says. We should be in the skies while the weather holds, the storm season will be upon us by the time our dear Captain gets us some real action again," said Robbie.

Maggie sidled up to him, "It won't be long now. Not if we--"

Robbie silenced her with a look, "Not here. We need to get the others onside first. But do it quietly."

Nessa waited until the three had left before making her way through the passage toward the Captain Duke's study. She opened the bookshelf as quietly as she could, but before she had set foot into the room, Trick's voice greeted her.

"Nessa, just in time for morning tea."

Trying to hide her guilty look behind the sweep of her blonde hair, Nessa strode in to sit by the hearth while Trick poured the tea service. Once they were settled in with warm scones, Trick nodded in her direction.

"Well, I wouldn't say sneaking about the Haven

constitutes bedrest, but it was an unlikely prospect to begin with. So, what did you learn?"

"Robbie's up to something."

"What a surprise."

"Renault and Maggie are in on it, there's likely others," she continued. "They'll try to recruit more."

"I expected as much. But the Captain wants proof before he proceeds. We need to know more about their plans."

The two of them plotted over their tea, drawing up plans for the most loyal of their crew to infiltrate Robbie's gang. They had just settled on the details when Cat and Mouse came bounding in, arms filled with packages, followed closely by the Captain Duke.

"Ness, why are you out of bed?"

Nessa ignored his question, "I see your trip to town was a success."

The Captain frowned and busied himself with the packages. Nessa saw Cat and Mouse exchange a significant look.

"Where is Clara?" she asked. "What did you do now?"

"Actually, nothing," he replied.

"Clara saw someone who might have recognized her, and now she's all afraid again," Cat blurted out.

"He barely saw her. She's safe here," said the Captain, but Nessa could see his concern.

"Well, then we need to make sure she knows that. Cat, Mouse, get your gear. Let's show her how to fight."

The siblings happily tumbled out of the study, racing towards the weapons room. Nessa stood and stretched. It would be good to get some fresh air.

"Are you sure about this?" Trick asked.

"Clara is not the same girl we found in that cargo hold. She needs a reminder of who she can be. If something from her past has spooked her, I figure we give her the tools to fight back," she explained. "She needs to trust in herself before she places her faith in the rest of us."

The Captain Duke considered her words and nodded, "You're right. Her training begins now. Teach her to fight, Nessa."

Nessa smiled and left the study, making her way slowly up the stairs to her rooms. She remembered the years before she'd chosen the pilot's life. It had been a long while since she'd had to be afraid. But she recognized those parts of herself in the young woman. It was time to turn the lady into a proper hellcat. With that, Nessa knocked on Clara's door...

Author's Note

I could spend days discussing all the historical quirks of our world. Names that were almost lost to dusty old books, stories of times gone by that escaped the accepted narrative. For every story we know it seems a thousand or more are lost, likely more.

One of the reasons that the steampunk genre fascinates me is the way it allows for stories to be reinserted into an epoch to create these days of future past. 'The greatest era that never was,' as described by some.

I do enjoy messing with the history books. How can one resist the delightful opportunity to envision a world that spun sideways from our own?

In the steampunk history of the Captain Duke, a royal declaration by Queen Victoria in 1866 that was intended to secure her hold on the throne after the death of her husband had the unintended consequence of legitimizing gender equality years before it actually happened in ours. The subsequent advancements in steam-powered and mechanized technology helped to put Britain at the forefront of global development, thanks to the doubling of its national brainpower as young women joined the ranks of engineers, scientists and inventors.

In our world, Queen Victoria did retreat from public life to mourn her husband, Albert, for many years. At one point a protestor even posted a sign on Buckingham Palace declaring it available for rent in her prolonged absence. She eventually returned to her duties and attended the opening of Parliament for the first time since Albert's death in 1866.

Queen Victoria did not need to issue a proclamation securing her throne. She did, however, support the passing of the Reform Act in 1867 that extended voting rights to many urban, working-class men. And yet, she was not a supporter of women's suffrage.

History can be disappointing.

Sometimes, one must look around the dusty edges of historical tomes to find the stories. You must search the empty margins of shiny textbooks. The stories are there; they want to be told. Stories that are real, and other fictions wrapped around a kernel of truth.

The Press and the Public Service by Eustace Clare Grenville Murray is a real book. A prolific writer with a scandalous career in diplomacy, he was also the natural son of a duke.

A favourite story of mine is that of Ada Lovelace (1815-1852). She is considered to be the first person in history to make the conceptual leap regarding the potential applications for Charles Babbage's analytical engine, and her work is the progenitor of our modern day computer coding. She was also, famously, the estranged daughter of Lord Byron. But Ada only lived to 36 years of age. Just imagine what our world might look like if she had a few more years and fewer constraints. She saw poetry in mathematics, and her brilliance shines through the ages.

Women like Ada Lovelace and her tutor, Mary Somerville (1780-1872), led the way for advanced female scholarship. Somerville and her contemporary, Caroline

Herschel (1750-1848), set a precedent for the fairer sex when they were both made honourary members of the Royal Astronomical Society in 1835.

In the steampunk universe of the Captain Duke, Somerville took advantage of Queen Victoria's declaration to fulfill a life-long dream of establishing a school for female scholars. Using her vast network of contacts, and drawing on the many bright young women she corresponded with over the years, Somerville considered this work to be her crowning achievement. She attended the matriculation of the first graduating class before her death. The school itself was named for her former student (and thanks to a generous donation from Ada's heirs).

Lovelace University—and the incredible Professor Sewell—will feature quite prominently in Book 3 of the Tales of the Captain Duke.

Everyone has a story. Thank you all for being part of mine. Until next time!

Rebecca Diem
May 2015

Acknowledgements

It pleases me greatly to be sharing my work with you once again. The past year has been quite the adventure, and I could not have done it without the many brilliant people I am humbled to have in my life.

Thank you to Arden Dier, Lori Steuart, and Gurushabd Khalsa for being my first readers and editors. The world of Clara and the Captain Duke is richer for having passed through your imaginations (and has many less typos).

My eternal gratitude to Maryann Thomas of The Ginger Press, Andrew Williamson of the Black Cat Artspace, Laura Sinclair, Antonio Carito, and Heather Mundle for your various parts in making a tri-city book tour happen for The Stowaway Debutante.

Thank you to Sarah Dier-McComb for her beautiful artwork on the cover once again, and to Steve Armstrong for bringing all the elements together for the design.

And finally, to my parents, Ray and Kelly, and my siblings, Andrew, Sarah and Leah. Thank you for sharing your time, your feedback, your enthusiasm, and your love. The more I grow and see the world, the more I realize how incredibly special our family is. You are so magnificent.

--Rebecca Diem
May 2015

Rebecca Diem grew up in a far-off land known as Chatsworth, Ontario, surrounded by hills and forests and streams and strange metal beasts that tore through the landscape leaving iron in their wake.

And one day she began to write it all down...

Web: rebeccadiem.com
Email: rebeccadiemauthor@gmail.com
Facebook: RebeccaDiemAuthor
Twitter/Instagram: @kthnxbex

Thank you so much for supporting my work.
Please share, rate and review!

20028298R00080

Made in the USA
Columbia, SC
09 September 2018